MAGIC BURN

SEDONA VENEZ

WANT FREE SEDONA VENEZ BOOKS?

Sign up for Sedona Venez's Newsletter and receive FREE BOOKS. In addition to the free stories, you will also get special pricing, exclusive previews and news of new releases.

GET A FREE SEDONA VENEZ BOOK!

Join Sedona's mailing list to be the first to know of new releases, free books, special prices and other author giveaways.

https://sedonavenez.com/free-book

🦋　I　🦋

"HEADS UP!" I shouted, amplifying my voice, so that it reverberated off the walls of the cave. Right on cue, all the supernaturals within range, the ones on our side of this bloody war, quickly moved out of the way. Within seconds, my dragon's flame incinerated a squadron of goblins. Their comrades shrieked in anger, and I deflected an incoming arrow with a deft flick of my hand.

Learning that deflection charm after the hive's first invasion, had come in handy time and time again. I was suddenly less annoyed at my older brother, Zayne, for making me sit through hours and *hours* of classroom time to learn spell theory. There hadn't been time for lessons in charms, spells, or magic of any kind since I was a teenager. After all, in another life, I was just a fae psychologist, living and working a simple life in New York City. My life there, was Friday night martinis with friends and nearly almost all of the rest of my time was spent with clients. Though, I occasionally met up with my fae sisters—no blood relation, of course—for a weekend of fae-induced frivolity. Ordinary. Drama-free. Peaceful.

Now, everything had changed. I was Kaye Allister, half-fae, half-dragon shifter, fighting a righteous war alongside my half-brother, Zayne, and his militia of supernatural resistance warriors.

Our goal: stop a bloodthirsty Archmage named Abramelin from eradicating shifter clans from the face of the planet.

One of our greatest assets?

My dragon.

My non-magical, surly, tongue-in-cheek, *swoon-worthy* dragon, Darius. He fought every skirmish in dragon form, which was no small task given he was the size of a city bus, and we fought in secret caverns, hidden beneath the supernatural realm of Alfheim.

Sometimes it was a tight fit, especially now that the curse of his ex-girlfriend—a witch, no less, both literally and figuratively —was finally broken, and he had full use of his wings. But I was always just a little more smitten with him after each battle. I couldn't help it. Darius in dragon form—with his scales, red as a summer sunset, and his flame, blue as a dying star—was the most exquisite thing I'd ever seen in my life.

No one could blame me for crushing hard on the guy. It wasn't every day that I got a chance to date a beautiful dragon shifter with a wicked sense of humor, right?

It certainly helped that he had been willing to give his life for mine when one of Abramelin's men tried to toss me from thirty feet up to what would have undoubtedly been sudden death. Yeah, I was *never* going to live that down.

Unfortunately, we'd had plenty of opportunities since that initial battle, between Abramelin's forces and Zayne's militia, for Darius to give his life for me. In the month that followed that skirmish, the hive—aptly named because the headquarters of Zayne's secret underground world was shaped like a beehive— had almost twelve raids. Some of them were noteworthy. Others, like the goblin siege today, were just a nuisance.

Still, no enemy force could be taken lightly. Abramelin was hell-bent on annihilating an entire race of supernatural beings—a race I'd only recently learned I was a part of, courtesy of my mom's affair with a dragon shifter. Even if I hadn't learned I was half-shifter, I still would have fought this battle, side-by-side with my older fae brother and my beautiful dragon, Darius, because it was the right thing to do. No one deserved Abramelin's level of persecution, of magical terrorism, solely because he or she happened to be born a shifter.

So, we would fight to the very end. Today's battle was just a drop in the shit-storm of conflict swirling around the supernatural community, all just outside the realm of human awareness.

Or so I hoped. I couldn't imagine what would happen if things spilled over and people found themselves forced to get involved. If humans did one thing well, it was nuking whatever potential threat they could, *before* said threat nuked them.

Literally.

"Kaye, behind you!" I whirled around at Zayne's prompting, nailing the goblin, who'd been creeping up behind me, square in the face with my foot. I would have preferred my fist—so much more satisfying—but given that most goblins weren't taller than hip-height, it was the best I could do. The creature emitted something that sounded like a belch, and I hit him with a disorienting hex—a flash of bright yellow from my fingertips. I followed that with another hex that was basically the magical version of get-the-fuck-out-of-my-face—a flash of red light. Seconds later, the little creature sailed across the cavern, hitting the huge, rough stone wall with a grunt.

The goblins had coordinated an attack with a handful of mountain trolls from Alfheim. The goblins were supposed to crush us with their magic. Unfortunately for them, goblin magic wasn't much to speak of, and their attack amounted to only a lot of green slime everywhere. While sticky, foul-smelling and quite slippery, it didn't do all that much damage in the grand scheme of things. Our fairies, elves, witches, dryads and even our one vampire had more magic in their pinkies, more spells in a single brain cell, than goblins had in their entire bodies.

The trolls were eliminated with a sunlight spell, turning them all to stone the second they came barreling into a cave we called Freedom Falls—because of the gorgeous waterfall, gushing down from the ceiling into an underground, blue lake. Intelligence had them arriving around noon; they didn't make it until two that afternoon, and we were ready. With the massive trolls hardened into decorative statues, it was just us and the goblins. It would have been an unfair fight, if they hadn't had the numbers. I'd never seen so many of the pesky fuckers in one place in all my life.

Goblins had the height advantage. They were quick, slippery and mischievous to a fault. All in all, however, *not* great fighters. As Darius stomped out a cluster of them, squishing them under his enormous dragon talons, the rest fled through the tunnel their trolls had carved. When the last one was gone, a fae and a witch got to work on closing the tunnel and sealing it with a ward. The rest of us checked on the wounded, piled up the dead goblins, and tried to get all the green slime off our boots.

While my right knee was a bit testy today, I'd managed to walk out of the battle unscathed—a far cry from my first rendezvous with Abramelin's forces. Either I was getting better, or his troops were getting less impressive with every wave we beat back. I wanted to think it was the former, but had a suspicion the latter would be better for the collective good.

"Good grief, man, put that thing *away*."

"No one's forcing you to look at it," Darius drawled from behind me, much to dwarf Alfred's disgust. A slow smile spread across my lips. "I can't help that he's at your eye level—"

Without looking back, I raised a hand and tried out the new summoning charm Zayne and I worked on last night. It was a blend of white magic and witchcraft, requiring the summoner to close her eyes, concentrate hard on the item in question, and then picture her white magic furling around it like a fist.

About thirty seconds later, a damp pair of jeans dropped into my outstretched hand. Apparently, *someone* had left them in any number of dank places around here; who knew underground caves could be so moist? Not I.

I turned around just as Alfred stalked by me, grumbling something about indecent exposure, and I had to swallow my laugh, knowing it wouldn't help the situation. Once fully turned around, I found my dragon in his human form—his delicious, gorgeous, *stunning* human form. Swallowing hard, I worked *very* hard on keeping my gaze level with his, my emerald green eyes fixed firmly on his stormy gray ones. Darius's brow quirked slightly, lips twisted into a wicked smirk, and I knew he was daring me to look down.

If I did, my gaze was bound to wander across the gorgeous muscular bounty of his body, over the hard planes and edges, right down to... Well, *it*.

Not today, bucko.

Rolling my eyes, I thrust his jeans at him, which he accepted with a long, drawn out sigh. I looked away while he shimmied into them. As soon as I heard his zipper whiz up, I crossed my arms and finally let myself look at him, ignoring the way my cheeks prickled with color.

"You okay?" I asked, assessing him for injuries. I'd gotten pretty good at healing him in the field when the need arose, but since the caliber of Abramelin's attacks had been hit and miss, I hadn't needed to heal him in a few weeks. Today appeared no different. While sweaty and a little soot-stained, Darius was in perfect condition.

"Fine," he told me, hands on his hips—and pectorals on full display.

Don't stare, Kaye. Don't. Do. It.

He shook his head. "Smells like shit in here though."

"Goblins." I rolled my eyes again. "Goblins and charred bodies. I'm not surprised it smells horrible."

We exchanged quick grins, though both faltered when one of Zayne's fae generals marched right up to us and thrust a pair of rubber gloves at each of us.

"Goblin slime is resistant to most magic," he remarked, evidently amused by our disgusted faces as we accepted our gloves. He then summoned a handful of garbage bags, a bucket, and a mop. "Unless you can heal, you're on cleaning duty."

"Oh, I can do that," I said quickly, as Darius started to protest. "I've been getting rather good at healing... It barely drains my energy anymore." Shoving my cleaning supplies into Darius's hands, I strode forward, headed for the gathering wounded, but was sure to shoot a smirk over my shoulder for my dragon. "Let's see this place sparkle."

He mouthed a very pleasant *fuck you* at me. I only laughed harder when he tried to shove his big hands into gloves that were obviously meant for me, then quickened my stride when he blew smoke out his nostrils, clearly unimpressed.

Maybe he'd think twice about tempting me with his magnificent body when we were around the rest of the militia.

I snorted. *Highly unlikely.*

~

"TODAY WAS NOTHING MORE THAN A DISTRACTION." I flinched when my brother's hand slammed down hard on his desk, hard enough to knock over a jar of quills and a pot of ink. He cursed, hastily gathering important documents, while I all but leaped out of my chair to contain the damage. Quills upright, I summoned a thick cloth and threw it over the spilled black ink. While I had many new spells, charms, and hexes in my arsenal, cleaning spells hadn't exactly been high on the priority list. Zayne would just have to clean it better when we left his chambers.

Darius remained unmoved, probably used to Zayne and me falling into the sibling routine more and more these days. He leaned against the stonework creeping up the wall around the fireplace. The mantel was made of a blend of crystal—infused with protective magic—and natural slate from the caves around the hive. It was a grand piece of design, but Darius would always draw my gaze first, not the masonry. He crossed his arms when our eyes met, much of the joking and silliness from our post-battle flirting gone. Zayne's ire had sucked all the fun out of the room in a heartbeat.

"What makes you say that?" I asked, settling down in the fat, yet stiff leather armchair. My eyes drifted to the map etched into the desk's wooden surface featuring both Alfheim and North America. I focused intently on where the two worlds intersected. I cleared my throat as my brother pushed his high-backed chair away and started pacing, hands clasped behind his back. "Today's battle was just like all the others—"

"They've all been distractions," he snapped. I didn't take offense to his tone. While we were only rekindling our relationship after years apart, I knew he had an insane amount of stress on his shoulders. After all, he was responsible for every living creature here—and, in his eyes, every supernatural and shifter in Alfheim and the human world. He led the resistance. He fought in every battle we did, usually leading the charge.

He was allowed to be a bit snappy and churlish. I could give him that, though I would put my foot down at outright rudeness. I mean, he had pulled *us* out of our cozy dinner up in my room for this little meeting.

"Abramelin's forces have been assaulting Alfheim as well, particularly in the Core," he told me after a few moments of tense pacing. I stiffened, a twinge of anxiety making my stomach turn.

"How... What's happening?"

"Guerilla-style attacks," my brother said, sighing. From the way he spoke, I could tell it pained him. "Hit and runs. Our forces outside can't keep up. It's not good. I believe he thinks he has weakened the supernatural community substantially enough, that he can finally unleash his wrath on the shifter clans."

Darius's growl told me he wasn't about to let that happen,

but I wasn't sure we had the ability to stop Abramelin from our location in the hive.

"I've only just heard from my intelligence agents that he's moving west."

I frowned. "Why west?"

"The clans," Darius answered for Zayne, his voice gruff. "There are several wolf and bear clans to the west, along with the dragon communities. They're very powerful."

"Indeed." Zayne nodded, his expression tight. "He'll want to weaken those more substantial clans before he delivers the killing blow. It is our estimation that once they are sure of a victory, they'll encircle the stronger shifter clans from all sides and eliminate them."

"That's horrible," I whispered. My words had no meaning anymore, everything Abramelin did was horrible. There were cubs in those clans. And the elderly. Shifters who had never fought a day in their lives. It wasn't fair to pit them against an army of supernatural magic-wielders, but it was evident that had been Abramelin's plan all along.

And, really, we had known that. We weren't fast enough to stop it.

"These little skirmishes have been distractions," Zayne insisted. "He's been keeping us busy down here, so we don't divert too many of our forces to Alfheim and the human world, where the real fighting will take place."

I stood, my heart racing. "We can't just sit here anymore."

"We need to warn them," Darius agreed.

"If we go now, maybe we can stop them," I continued, pushing some scraps of parchment aside on Zayne's desk to get a better look at the maps. "It will take time to move all those supernaturals into place. If we can—"

"Abramelin will take advantage of the portals," Zayne remarked, scowling. "He'll move quickly. Quicker than we've been giving him credit for lately."

"Then we need to move faster," Darius said as he stalked

across the dimly lit room and stood by my side. I caught the slight shake of Zayne's head, but before he could shoot my dragon down, I offered a better solution.

"We should split up," I told them, my voice soft as I contemplated the near future. "Darius and I can make our way toward the clans in the west, with a group of fighters, of course, and you can take others to warn the remainder of the clans. Abramelin may think he's killed or weakened enough supernaturals to make a move, but we have a decent sized militia here, Zayne. We could do this."

I glanced at Darius to gauge his reaction. While he still wore a hard expression, he started to nod, his stormy gray eyes distant and reflective. As always, my dragon was on my side. Squaring my shoulders and drawing in a deep breath, I turned my attention to Zayne, who seemed less sold on the idea than I'd hoped.

"The portals will still be faster—"

"Then *we* can use the portals, for goodness sake," I fired back, arms crossed. "We have to do *something*. We need to warn those clans about this. Who has the strength and magic to combat Abramelin if he's already out there? We do. We can handle whatever he throws at us along the way."

His arms fell to his side as he studied me, his frown darkening, and I shifted my weight back and forth between each leg, under his stare.

"I never wanted this for you," he admitted with a shake of his head. "I didn't want to involve you—"

"Well, the time for that is long gone," I told him. "I'm here. I've been fighting, and I'm going to keep fighting until one-half of our supernatural community isn't on the brink of extinction from a hateful bigot." There it was again—that flash of pain across his features, like he temporarily couldn't handle the fact that his little sister was here. Well, he was just going to have to get used to it. *What was the point of his magic lessons, if he didn't want me to take an active role in all this?* I lifted my chin slightly, determined. "Deal with it, Zayne."

Darius chuckled under his breath, looking away so my brother wouldn't see his delight in my saucy attitude. A little half-smile crossed my lips too, but I wasn't quite as gleeful as my dragon. After all, did I *really* want to trek across the human world from shifter clan to shifter clan? No. Especially not after learning I was half-shifter myself. The whole subject was still too touchy, too fresh, for me to tackle right now. However, if I threw myself to the wolves, metaphorically and literally, then I would probably have to deal with some things sooner than I was ready for.

But there were more important things out there, of course, than my issues with my heritage and the secrets my family kept. Lives were at stake. We *had* to do this.

"Fine." Zayne returned to his desk in a huff, trailing a finger over the various routes on his map. "But we'll need to stop in Alfheim before we go. Abramelin's been hammering it relentlessly over the last few days, and it's time to do a bit of damage control..."

$\maltese$ 2 $\maltese$

HAMMERING ALFHEIM relentlessly was probably the biggest fucking understatement I'd ever heard in my life. The place was in absolute ruin when we emerged from our little underground sanctuary. Abramelin and his men had decimated it. Whole forests were nothing but ash and cinder now. Scorched earth now had a whole new meaning to me, as I took in what was once the most exquisite realm I had ever seen. While the forests had been devastated, many we passed were already experiencing new growth, fueled by the innate magic of the woods and those who dwelled within.

The Core was another story entirely. Before our merry band of traveling militia fighters even hit the city, we could tell the place had been ransacked. While there were no active fires, smoke spires twirled up toward an otherwise beautifully clear, blue sky. Once, the Core had been littered with apartment towers, both floating and anchored to the ground. Now many of the taller ones were no longer standing—at least, not at their full heights. It was like someone had swung a sword and chopped the entire city in half.

How had we not known all this was going on? While we tried our hardest to survive below ground in our immense caverns with plunging waterfalls and glittering lakes lined with diamonds, the core population of Alfheim suffered.

Before we left, my brother told me he had people up here, trying to help the weak and injured while rallying the strong to fight, but nothing much had come of their efforts. Most of Zayne's forces, Darius and myself included, had been tied up with attack after attack at the hive and the surrounding living quarters. We'd been too busy trying to keep the devils out, that we missed them annihilating one of our biggest assets behind our backs.

"It looks bad," Darius acknowledged. We walked side-by-side near the front of the pack, Zayne leading the charge way up at the head. When I didn't respond right away, he clasped my hand and pulled me closer, pressing a rare, tender kiss to my temple. I tore my eyes from the smoldering remains of the Core with some difficulty, meeting his gaze as he said, "This will fuel people to join the cause. Those who want revenge will join our ranks."

"So, this was a *good* thing?"

"No," he insisted quickly. I knew I'd only said the words because it was either lash out angrily or buckle down and cry. Darius sighed and lifted his gaze back to the city, wearing enough of a scowl for both of us. "This is a tragedy. All we can do now is hope it will help our cause."

I knew that, of course. I only wished it hadn't come to such dire straits in order to pad the militia with revenge-driven super- naturals. After all, this whole damn thing had started with revenge; I couldn't fathom that particular motivation making many of the new recruits disciplined and rational. We didn't need someone losing his cool, *especially* with the lives of so many shifters on the line.

Not that I could blame them. The Core was a mess. We could all see it, even as Zayne stopped the marching horde before entering the city to issue his orders. If the architecture of the city had taken such a hit, I couldn't imagine what had become of its people. The thought made my palms sweaty, and I pulled my hand out of Darius's so I could cross my arms. I knew many within the Core. Friends. Fae sisters. Our cell phones didn't work down here, so I couldn't connect with them that way, nor did I have any magical communication devices handy.

I was in the dark. I had no idea who was alive or dead—and to think, yesterday we were having a merry old time punting goblins around a cave, joking about Darius's nudity. It all seemed so...cavalier now. The little permanent knot of guilt in my stomach tightened, as I started to spiral down into the depths of my thoughts, fearing the worst.

"Kaye." The sharpness in Zayne's tone brought me back, sounding as though he'd tried to get my attention a few times already. Suddenly he was only a few feet away, and factions of his militia were already moving into the Core. I frowned. *How long had I been mentally churning through worst case scenarios?*

"You and Darius are with me," my brother—half-brother, I ought to be used to it by now—told me, assessing me with a faint hint of concern. I nodded, not wanting him to send me back or make me wait outside the Core limits, because he thought I couldn't handle what might be inside.

"Right. Cool."

I caught Darius shooting me a sidelong glance. Okay. Maybe *cool* wasn't the most appropriate response. But Zayne had already moved on, his posse of captains and generals following at his heels, and instructed a band of elfin warriors to sweep the forests and find volunteer recruits.

When the talks were complete, most of the militia split off into separate groups, leaving about thirty of us to follow Zayne directly into the city. I shouldered my way through the crowd and strode along behind Zayne, Darius was behind me glaring down any who objected. My half-brother chatted softly with one of his generals, hands clasped behind his back and features furrowed. There was no time for him to hold my hand—not that I wanted him to, anyway.

We crossed the barrier between the outer limits, the suburbs mostly, and the Core's downtown area, and for once, the chaos reminded me of that which I'd experienced my first day at the hive. Although the city had been decimated and the people were dirty, there was non-stop movement. Children ran rampant, their schoolhouses most likely destroyed or shut down. Shopkeepers still peddled their wares, but it was obvious their hearts weren't in it. Window ledges lacked their vibrant floral arrangements, and no advertisements shouted at us as we walked by. The Core felt both subdued and fettered with nervous energy.

It made my stomach turn. I couldn't imagine living here in this.

As we passed, much to my surprise, men and women of all supernatural races dropped whatever they were doing and joined us. Our group of thirty almost doubled along the path to the high council buildings in the center of the Core. It was clear that those who remained within the city knew all about Zayne's militia—and probably thought they should have joined sooner. Those who fell in line beside us were welcomed with broad smiles, back claps, and handshakes. Those who stared us down, with eyes narrowed and mouths pinched, were ignored.

It wasn't our fault that Abramelin had gone totally ballistic up here. At least we were trying to *do* something about him. At least we weren't just burying our heads in the sand and pretending everything was fine.

I didn't blame those who didn't want to fight alongside us, but the glares were uncalled for, as was the spitting. A few spat at our feet as we passed, but Zayne ordered those who tried to engage to stand down. We weren't here to cause more drama.

"Kaye!" A strangled cry from one of the side streets caught my attention, but while I stopped, the militia members around me kept moving. Darius's frame managed to shield me, forcing people to walk around us, rather than knock into us. I tried to see over the crowd, but only once they all passed, was I able to spy who had shouted for me.

"Catriona!" Fae speed propelled me forward, turning me into

nothing but a blur to onlookers until I collided with my fae sister —one of my best friends, in fact. We grasped each other like centuries had passed, clinging to one another, hard and tight. I could feel her slim figure trembling against me as we buried our faces in each other's hair. I closed my eyes as relief coursed through my veins. She smelled like smoke, a scent so unbecoming for a fae as beautiful as she. Her platinum blonde locks were slightly matted, and as I opened my eyes to hazard a peek down her back, I noted that she was dirty, like she had been hands-on in the Core's rebuilding efforts.

"I've been so worried," she whispered in my ear, hugging tighter than I thought possible. I gave her shoulder a squeeze, then pulled back to get a better look into her ice blue eyes. To others, they might appear cold, but to me those stunning orbs had always been the epitome of comfort and love. I clasped her face with both hands, my eyes filling with tears, and hastily kissed her cheeks before dragging her into another hug.

"What are you *doing* here?" I hissed. "You're supposed to be in New York!"

We broke apart, and Catriona wiped the stream of tears rushing down her cheeks away. Both of us sniffled, my rush of protective anger fading fast.

"I came looking for *you*," she told me, her words followed shortly by a strangled laugh. "Belladonna told me you were staying at her place and I was welcome to join you if I wanted to. Then I heard rumors of that *man*, that Archmage, and I had to pull you out!"

"Oh, Catriona, I wasn't even *in* the Core when all this—"

"I hoped not," she insisted, voice high, almost panicked. I stroked her cheeks again, wishing her some relief—wondering if I ought to infuse her with a bit of my white magic. She felt like she needed it as she pressed on. "I arrived the day before all... *this* happened. I've been trying to survive ever since. Helping others. Fighting off rogue demons. Rebuilding. Belladonna's apartment was totally destroyed."

"Is Belladonna okay?" I asked hastily at the sight of tears welling in her eyes. "She wasn't—"

"She's in the human realm," Catriona told me, wiping under her eyes and taking a few deep breaths. "She and Lily and Rose are fine. From what I last heard, they were hopping on Bella's boat and sailing as far from all this, as possible. Maybe Bali. I don't know. She has houses everywhere."

That she did. Belladonna was like a surrogate mother to me, a fae of immense power with two beautiful daughters who I looked to as sisters, blood ties or not. She spent half the year in Alfheim and half the year vacationing around the human world. I never knew where the lovely woman got all her money from, to do as she pleased, but at that moment, I was grateful for her seemingly endless funds. At least she could keep her daughters and other supernaturals safe from Abramelin, if she stayed out of the conflict.

"And the others?" I asked, thinking about the many fae I knew, that were in danger, if they didn't head for cover. Catriona hiccupped, but seemed to be calming down.

"Headed for the mountains," she told me. "They asked me to join them, but I wanted to find you first."

"Except Jasmine, I'm sure," I said without thinking. Catriona's dark brows shot up, her eyes widening a bit, and I shrugged. Jasmine was a fae like us, but if this were high-school, she would be the ringleader of the pretentious bitch clique. A total mean girl. "What? You know she spouts anti-shifter sentiments whenever she gets the chance. I'm sure Abramelin recruited her in a heartbeat."

Not that I had any real proof—just a hunch, based on the kind of person Jasmine was, and a strong dislike for her character. It wouldn't have surprised me in the slightest if she agreed with everything that Abramelin was doing. Hell, for all I knew, she was fighting alongside him.

But then again, she'd always made a fuss about getting her

hands dirty. Maybe she *was* hiding away with the others, using the safety of the group to protect herself from breaking a nail.

"Ladies," my dragon's voice rumbled in my ear. I practically jumped out of my skin when I felt his warm hand slide around my hip. "Maybe we ought to take this conversation somewhere a little more private?"

While Catriona ogled Darius like he had six heads, I scanned the alley we found ourselves in and quickly agreed. While there were, dwarves wearing high council pendants—a sign they were hired by the city—working all around us, there were also a number of other supernaturals who seemed far too interested in our conversation for comfort.

"I have a place we can go," Catriona offered after a slight pause. "It's not much, but it's definitely private..."

"I'VE ALWAYS THOUGHT YOU WERE ONLY HALF FAE," CATRIONA admitted as she refilled our tea cups. I watched the steam swirl up in beautiful ribbons, heat darkening my cheeks as she chattered on. "I mean, I assumed you just didn't want to tell me for some reason so I didn't want to bring it up."

"What? No, I had no idea," I said stiffly as I returned my little cup on its plate. Beside me, Darius looked ridiculous, slurping his lavender-scented tea from such a tiny mug, but his aura suggested he was all right with it. Calm. Alert, but not on edge. "Why did you think that?"

Catriona smiled as though it was the most obvious answer it the world. "You're just different from us," she replied, shrugging her shoulders. Then she saw the look of uncertainty on my face and her eyes softened. "In a good way, Kaye. You aren't exactly a typical fairy."

Catriona's private place was a room in one of the few undamaged hotels in the Core. It was stationed near the high council buildings. While Darius had dipped over to let Zayne know where we were, I took the time to fill my best friend in on all the bullshit that had happened to me over the last few weeks. She was horrified by most of it, though she continued to be the dutiful hostess, refilling our tea cups and sharing her food supplies —cured meats and fae bread. The only thing she hadn't flipped her lid about, was the fact that I was a fae-shifter hybrid. I was thankful for that, since Darius had returned just as I told her.

"It's nothing to be ashamed of," Catriona insisted, taking a seat on the little twin-sized bed while Darius and I occupied the two-seater couch near the door. "I have a great aunt who married a bear shifter way back in the day. There's more crossing over between supernaturals and shifters than people think. I guess it's still taboo, though."

"Clearly," Darius grunted with a nod to the window. Catriona gulped noticeably, still awkward in my dragon's presence, like she wasn't sure what to make of him.

"Well, it's stupid," she said, this time more firmly. "Don't let it get to you, Kaye. You're still the same person you've always been. Now you have a whole new family to explore, and that's *wonderful*. It's more people to love."

My lips twitched into a smile. "That's a nice way to look at it, I guess. I hadn't considered that."

"You should." She sat up straighter. "I'm sure they're lovely. Besides, some of the best people I know are shifters or part-shifter, you included. I think it's great." Catriona bit her lip as Darius and I drank our tea, both of us sensing she had more to say. "And... I think it's awful what Abramelin has done. I want to help you and your brother. I want to fight."

I hesitated, slowly setting my cup back down on its saucer and sighing. Catriona was such a little thing. Angelic. Soft. Feminine. I knew she had power in her own right, but the thought of putting her on the battlefield... Well, it terrified me.

Darius, however, seemed to see none of that. He grinned at

my best friend, gray eyes swimming with a newfound respect, and nodded.

"We'll be happy to have you."

"With us," I said quickly, hating how happy Catriona looked to be joining a militia. I wanted her safe, not in the middle of the fray. But as soft and sweet and demure as she could be, if alcohol wasn't involved, my best friend was stubborn as a mule and usually got her way. If she was joining this fight, then I wanted her where I could watch her at all times.

"Absolutely," Catriona said brightly. "When do we start?"

"Now," Darius said, talking over me. "Zayne wants us back at the high council buildings as soon as possible. We'll be heading back to the human world today."

So soon? I swallowed hard as we stood and helped Catriona pack up her things. Before, I'd wanted to get out of Alfheim immediately; there was no time to rest with Abramelin closing in on northern and western shifter clans. But now that it was happening, so fast, and my best friend getting sucked into the action, I wasn't sure I was ready.

And, I also couldn't decide whether or not that made me a coward.

"Are you sure you can do this?" Zayne asked, his voice hushed. I shot him a narrowed look. Even if I wasn't sure, that didn't matter at this point. It had all been decided for me, without me, and if I backed out now, I was *definitely* a coward.

"Yeah, I'm good," I said. I adjusted the cloak hanging over my shoulders—a royal purple one, matching my half-brother's, to indicate my rank within the militia. When Zayne continued to stare at me with that questioning expression, I huffed and pushed at his shoulder, forcing a smile. "Seriously. I'm fine. It's not like I'm doing this alone, or anything. Darius is with me, which I think bodes better for us than it does for you."

After all, Darius was the only shifter in this army—and now we were heading out into shifter territory. Zayne was leading a force north to warn the wolf clans there, and to also start crafting protective magical barriers to hopefully keep Abramelin's forces out. Timing would be key: they had to make sure they reached the clans before Abramelin did. I, meanwhile, had troops of my own to look after, as I went west with Darius and Catriona in tow. There were bear and dragon clans to warn. Catriona had volunteered to craft the wards at each location. Once we had warned everyone and gathered whatever fighters we could—Darius's job, to persuade them to fight—we would meet with Zayne in the Rockies where the mountain range crossed over Montana, Wyoming, and Idaho to regroup.

"Don't do anything reckless," Zayne muttered as I shouldered my pack. Behind me, my very own troops—somehow, I was qualified to lead them, though I suspected it was because Zayne and I were family and nothing more—were loading up, ready to make the first jump through the portals to western US shifter clan territory.

"This whole endeavor is reckless," I told him, "but I won't take any unnecessary risks."

Not with Catriona as part of my company. I'd already scolded Darius for so readily accepting her, and he promised he would keep a watchful eye on her when I couldn't.

Then, much to my surprise, Zayne kissed me on each cheek, then my forehead, before rallying his band of supernaturals. Squaring my shoulders, I watched him go, leading them through one of the dozens of portals out of Alfheim. After they were gone, I felt the eyes of my troops watching me, close to fifty supernaturals in total, and I gulped.

"Okay… guys," I managed, not entirely comfortable with my current level of authority, but I knew there was nothing I could do about it. So, I decided my best strategy was just to be myself. I nodded to the portals. "Let's go save some lives."

"ALL IN FAVOR of sending the dragon up to do an aerial sweep, raise your hands."

Well, fuck. I'd already lost control of my troops, and we hadn't even reached the first shifter clan. I planted my hands on my hips and watched as most of those present lifted one hand. While a few looked determined, grim even, probably about my stubborn refusal to just *use* Darius whenever anyone else wanted, a few had the decency to at least look a little guilty about going against my orders. Catriona stood a few feet from me, her arms crossed as she glowered at the traitors.

It wasn't *quite* that dire. I didn't mind the use of democracy in my troops—but I would have preferred the final say in all things Darius-related. He had already expressed his concerns about rising above the tree line, fearing the risk of being spotted should Abramelin have any scouts patrolling the skyways. We were in the middle-of-nowhere Michigan, in one of the state's twenty *million* acres of forest—a fact we all had a chuckle about for some reason the first night we camped out after traveling between Alfheim and the human world.

Thankfully, seeing as we were nowhere near booming civilization, we could use our magic a little more freely. A few of our resident white witches had offered to use a cloaking spell to hide Darius if he stayed above a certain height, and everyone else wanted him to fly ahead to ensure our next portal destination was safe to use.

There were *many* portals around the country. A minimum of two in each state, with more unsanctioned ones cropping up every day, given the current political climate in the supernatural world. However, not every portal took you somewhere you wanted to go.

For example, the one that took us to a middle-of-nowhere forest in Michigan wouldn't take us far enough to reach the first clan on our list. So, we had to hike, the whole militia in tow, through the woods to the next portal destination. They'd all take us back to Alfheim when programmed to, but traveling around the human world just *had* to be more complicated than that.

Six creatures present could vanish from sight and reappear at another location—witches, mages, and two elves skilled in the craft. Unfortunately, that sort of teleportation usually required the magic user to know intimate details about the place he or she was transporting to. As of that moment, no one in my company had more than a basic understanding of the portal we were headed toward. We all knew it was at the base of a yew tree, one that would be marked with familiar runes that most supers knew marked it as a portal. Supposedly, there were signs leading up to its location—that and we'd all feel its presence as we drew nearer.

Well, most of us would. Darius, being a shifter, would be immune to its magical pull, though I knew his heightened senses would work in our favor regardless.

Even without magic, my dragon had a lot of value—yet another reason, I wasn't keen on sending him above the canopy and out of sight so that he could scout ahead. We had been doing pretty well for ourselves on foot, honestly.

"Guys, can we just talk about this more?" I asked, trying not to sound too whiny. After all, I was supposed to be in charge here, but two of my brother's captains—fairies from ancient families—seemed keen on sharing power.

With each other. Not with me.

"We've talked about it at length," Galen remarked with a sigh. His soft brown hair, like that of a sapling's trunk, fluttered gently in a breeze. He was a handsome fae—I'd seen many creatures making eyes at him—but I wished he'd address me with just a hint more respect. "The pros, the cons. We've talked about it. Now we've voted. It's been decided, Kaye."

Just as I opened my mouth to argue, Darius grumbled, "I guess the fucking tribe has spoken," before storming off into the trees. Exhaling deeply, I pinned Galen with a narrowed look, as the rest of the militia members dispersed behind him, clearly believing they had won some victory.

"Just because he's a shifter, doesn't mean you can order him around," I hissed in a low voice. My accusation made Galen produce the biggest eye roll I'd ever seen in my life.

"That's not what I'm doing. No one thinks that. He's an asset—"

"He's a friend," I countered tersely.

"He can be both," the fae captain told me with a frown. He folded his arms as his gaze swept up and down my figure—not in a leering sort of way, but as though he were assessing my fortitude. "You have to start looking at people as assets. We all are. That's why we're here. If you want to lead this squad—"

"Okay, okay," I muttered, waving him off. "I'll make sure he's doing it."

Not wanting Darius to get too far ahead, I hurried after him, Catriona at my heels, and found him stripping down in a small clearing.

"Oh," Catriona squeaked. When I glanced back, she had pointedly turned the other way—something I knew was for my benefit, not Darius's. Although I hadn't gone into detail about our make-out session after Abramelin's first attack on the hive, my best friend must have clued into the fact that Darius and I were a thing by now. I wanted to come right out and say it, but at this point, I wasn't even sure if I was ready to admit it to myself, much less Catriona. So, I left her there with her back turned, and stalked through the forest undergrowth, gritting my teeth when something prickly caught on my pants.

"You don't *have* to—"

"I don't want to ruffle feathers," Darius told me stiffly. "I'll do it. I think it's a stupid idea, but I'll do it. Once we reach the clans, all of them are going to be asking me for favors. *Asking.* Not telling. I can wait until then to outvote them, too."

Huh. Maybe not the healthiest attitude to have when it came to one's teammates, but I made a note to talk to him about it later. And maybe I'd talk to Galen and Quell, my two power-hungry fae captains, about *asking* Darius to do things, rather than having a majority vote force him into action when he clearly wasn't comfortable.

"Thank you," I said, keeping my gaze on his face as he unzipped his pants and wrenched them down his tree-trunk thighs. "I mean, for this doing this. I appreciate it."

"You don't even want me to do it."

"I—"

"Don't let them boss you around, Kaye," he murmured. "Just because they have some stupid rank in, let's face it, a ragtag army of misfits, doesn't mean they can order you around. Your brother put *you* in charge during his absence."

I bit my lip, almost feeling as though he blamed me for how things had turned out. If I had just put my foot down, he wouldn't be doing this—an attitude that also wasn't helpful. I swallowed my questions, tucking the psychologist in me away once more, figuring it wasn't worth the fight right now.

"At the first sign of danger, turn back," I told him instead, easing away to give him space to shift. "Don't do anything that will get you hurt."

"I think we've established how difficult that is," he fired back, smirking. Then, in two blinks, his human form transformed into his stunning dragon self, a creature who always took my breath away.

"Wow..." I jumped at the sound of Catriona's voice in my ear, soft and melodic—the complete opposite of the vibe Darius radiated with his sun-kissed scales and immense black claws and tail spikes. I shot her a grin, almost proud that she thought he was beautiful too. She held out her arm. "Would he mind if I, er, touched him? I've never seen a dragon in person. His scales..."

"Breathtaking, huh?"

"Absolutely."

Although I swore I saw Darius roll his eyes at Catriona's request, I motioned for him to wait two seconds—was he seriously in such a hurry to get into the sky after the fit he just threw—and told her to go right ahead. Beaming, she strode forward and caressed the scales creeping over his shoulders with the backs of her knuckles—then leaped away with a shriek.

"He burned me!" she cried, staggering into me. Sure enough, her skin blistered, white and juicy looking, as if she'd touched a scalding hot, stove burner.

"I can heal that," I insisted, shooting Darius a glare. *Had he known that would happen? And why hadn't it ever happened to me?* I touched him all the time in dragon form.

Was it because of my half heritage? Maybe only fellow dragon shifters could touch dragons—at least, not without singing their fingers as Catriona had done.

"Just go," I snapped when Darius huffed at me, a rush of black smoke shooting out his nostrils—almost in an *I told you so* sort of way, despite the fact he hadn't said anything to me. Because I didn't want those to be my last words to him before he shot off into dangerous territory, I added, "Be safe."

The ground shuddered as he took flight, two flaps of his enormous wings practically bending the century-old trees around us in half. Once he was gone, I hastily fueled Catriona's burns with a dose of white magic and a dash of healing energy. The gesture left me light-headed and weak-kneed, but with her hand healed, she held me steady until the world righted itself again.

"Thank you," she whispered. "Does Darius burn you too?"

"Not physically," I said, testing my balance out as I peered up at the blue, slightly cloudy sky. "Not yet, anyway."

Why weren't the witches shielding him? I could see my dragon, plain as day, from the clearing: he didn't exactly blend in with a baby blue background. Just as I was about to tell Catriona to run back and instruct the witches in question, to uphold their end of the bargain, Darius emitted an earthshattering bellow, one that rumbled the ground even harder than his take-off had. Both of us clamped our hands over our ears, wincing our way through the cry—until I finally realized what the issue was.

Within a minute or so of Darius shooting up into the sky, he was besieged with Abramelin's minions. There were so many that they blotted out the sun, like they'd been waiting for us. Gargoyles, for the most part.

"Come back!" I shouted, amplifying my voice and tapping into my enhanced sight to get a better view of things. Most of the goon squad had weapons in hand, and I thought back to the gargoyle attack at the train station—a blade of iron had managed to pierce through Darius's armor-like scales. We couldn't risk it here. With Catriona already racing back to warn the others, I cupped my hands around my mouth and shouted his name. Fire was his response, a blue blaze cutting through his enemies, but there were too many of them. Like a swarm of ants, they surrounded him, and when I saw him diving back for the forest, I knew, he finally realized he was outnumbered.

Amidst the gargoyles, was a sight I never thought I'd see: actual witches on *actual* broomsticks. *Was Abramelin forcing everyone to live up to their stupid stereotypes over at Camp Bigot or what?*

I scrambled out of the way as Darius's enormous dragon form slammed into the ground. When the dust cleared, he was human again, hastily shoving himself back into his clothes. I rushed forward to provide some cover, shooting a few easy hexes up at the gargoyles who decided to start dive-bombing him. They dodged the first two, but a violent streak of red, bright like freshly spilled blood, nailed one dead center in its chest. The creature exploded seconds later, and that sent his buddies scurrying back to the safety of the sky.

Right up to alert the circling witches.

"Come on," I urged, grabbing Darius's hand and dragging him toward the trees, knowing we'd need them for cover. "I can't out-hex a bunch of witches."

Sure, I was dipping into their magical realm of expertise with all the new spells and whatnot in my arsenal, but those broads had been practicing for years now. I only had a month under my belt, really, and I'd be outmatched in a hot second.

An old maple tree splintered into a thousand tiny pieces as we raced by, a pursuing witch's spell hitting that instead of us. Darius yanked me to the side to avoid the spray of wood chunks, both of us tumbling to the ground. He dragged me close, then threw himself on top of me until it stopped raining tree trunk and squirrel guts. Bits of coarse undergrowth poked into my face and hands. I gulped down a lungful of sweet, fresh air when Darius finally lifted off me. The witch hovered nearby, cackling —yet another stereotype—and I hurled a hex her way. The green flash of light was supposed to make her flesh erupt with blisters and boils, but she dodged it with a snarl and raised a hand at me, a bright yellow light surging to life within her palm.

Before she could launch it our way, with me already trying to summon up a defensive shield to protect us from whatever horror she had in store, her broom disappeared. She screeched as she plummeted toward the ground, and as I straightened up, I spied the cavalry charging in.

Although there were unsaid power struggles between myself and the other fae captains, at least I could count on everyone having my back when it mattered.

"The skies aren't safe," I said, as Galen rushed forward and extended a hand to help me up. Behind me, a band of our own witches chased Abramelin's men back to the clearing, the woods alight with sparks of magical color.

"Just like I said they wouldn't be," Darius added, getting up on his own and dusting his pants off. "It was clear when I went up, but they swarmed me within a minute or two."

"We need to get to the portal," Galen said firmly. "We don't have the numbers to fight. Those gargoyles... There must be at least two hundred of them up there."

"Then let's move." I pushed by him and willed a pulse of magic—a harmless nothing, really, just a hum of energy—to wash over the troops. "We're on the defense! No offensive procedures. Priority is to reach the portal before more of these assholes arrive!"

While it didn't appear that everyone agreed with my decree, they hightailed it back into the woods when it became clear that both Galen and Quell were on my side. I ordered the two fae to take up the front of the group, while Darius and I remained at the rear. Catriona stayed with us, despite my telling her to find a spot somewhere in the middle, but the longer we ran, the more thankful I was to have another magic wielder by my side.

Because apparently, Abramelin's gargoyles and witches weren't content to stick to the sky. Oh no. They tried to follow us into the trees. While Catriona, myself, and a gaggle of white witches fended off the spell-work of the enemy as best we could, the forest did the rest. Almost all the gargoyles were too big to fit between the trees, nor were they agile enough to dodge whatever was in their way. Darius managed to drag a few down and yank their heads clean off, yet most ended up trapped in branches or disintegrating when they slammed into sturdy tree trunks, the kind that could take a bit of a beating and still stay upright.

Our issue that afternoon was the sheer volume of enemy fire we had to deal with. They were everywhere, coming in from above, trying to take us out through the canopy. We ended up running for the better part of the afternoon, until the sun was on the far west of the forest, casting lengthy shadows across the trees. Hell, we'd been in such a hurry to get out and avoid being totally overrun, that we ended up leaving a lot of our gear behind.

The group slowed from a full-tilt run to a loping jog then to a slow walk when we happened upon another large clearing—and overhead, the skies were empty. I planted my hands on my hips, panting hard, and studied the sky for any signs of gargoyles or witches. Nothing. *When had they stopped tracking us?*

Judging from the murmurs rippling through the militia, everyone was on the same wavelength. *So, where the hell had they gone?*

With sweat dribbling down the sides of my face, I worked my way to the front of the pack, continuously scanning the crowd to make sure no one was injured. Besides minor bumps and bruises, folks seemed to be in good shape—though we were missing about five people. Just as I reached Galen and Quell, a crippling bout of cold crept up my body, starting at my feet and crawling up my legs. I hugged myself, teeth chattering, and lifted my gaze to the forest ahead of us.

No wonder Abramelin's men had stopped following us.

"What's up?" Darius asked, sounding slightly winded himself. He looked from me to the trees, then back again. "Why did we stop?"

"Can't you feel it?" Galen snapped before I could ask. "The cold?"

"Dragons burn hot, friend," Darius grunted—clearly, he hadn't let bygones be bygones yet with the whole vote thing. "What am I supposed to be feeling?"

"Dark magic," I told him. He frowned down at me, then pulled me close, an arm around my shoulder, and started to rub whatever parts of me his hand could reach. It helped, though his skin felt more fiery than usual in the presence of such bleak magic. It drifted out of the woods like a dark fog, sweeping over us, both beckoning unfamiliar travelers closer and warning others to steer clear.

"We're at the eastern entrance of the Hallowed Forest," Quell informed us, and the name sent heated whispers throughout the group. "The portal is on the other side."

"Hallowed Forest?" Darius continued to rub me, keeping the chill at bay. "What the hell is that? I mean, I can make deductions from the name, but—"

"You don't know *Hallowed Forest*?" Galen demanded, to which my dragon scoffed, a whiff of black smoke surging from his nostrils. I slid my arm around his waist and pinched, a silent warning to watch his temper with the fae captain. Things were stressful enough as it was.

"Sorry, I'm not up to date on all the hip supernatural lingo," Darius drawled. His voice had lost its edge, thank goodness. "No. I don't know the name of every forest in the fucking—"

"It's a dark forest," I said quickly, shrugging his arm off and taking a few steps closer. From here, it appeared quite normal, but unlike the other woodland terrain we had trekked through, shadow obstructed us from seeing too deeply into the trees. Sunlight didn't pierce the canopy—and that chill, that straight-to-the-marrow cold, was hard to ignore. I swallowed hard, stiffening when a figure darted between the trees, then vanished. "It's said to be haunted. Full of malevolent spirits. Ghosts. Dark creatures who couldn't find a home in Alfheim." I turned back to the captains. "We should go around."

"That was the original plan," Quell said with a glare toward the sky, "but Abramelin's goons sent us off-course."

"Like they were herding us here," I said, more to myself than my companions. The whispers of the militia had escalated to full-blown conversations, most of which sounded in favor of going around, not through.

"If that *was* Abramelin's plan, then he succeeded," Galen insisted, lifting his voice to quiet the others. "He wanted to put us behind and get to the portal first. We're losing time and daylight. I say we go through."

The uproar from the troops was the loudest yet, as we debated back-and-forth about which course to take. In the end, however, majority vote decided we'd go through the forest. I didn't want to; Hallowed Forest had a seedy reputation that made my toes curl. But Galen was right. We were wasting valuable time. Lives were at stake. We were supernaturals, magically-gifted. We could get through it, *if* we stuck together and worked as a team to repel whatever might try to stop us. According to the map, it would only take a few hours to cross.

"Yeah, but it's what the map *doesn't* show that scares me," an elf muttered to her brother, who nodded, eyes wide and bow loaded.

Darius, Catriona, and I exchanged wary looks, then hung back as Galen and Quell led the others into the woods. Taking up the rear, the three of us fanned out with Darius in the middle, and slowly made our way toward the trees.

The second I stepped past the first one, my breath fogged in front of me. Darius inhaled sharply as if feeling the forest's chill for the first time, and Catriona was as white as a ghost.

Fantastic.

☙   4   ❧

"SOMEONE REMIND me again why this was such a good idea?"
Catriona whimpered. My eyes narrowed at the trio in front of us
—an elf, a dwarf, and a dryad—who had spent the last ten
minutes whispering about the horrors of Hallowed Forest. *Sure,
the stories creeped me out too. Did I want to turn around and run back
for the safety of the outside world? Yup.* But this was the path we had
all agreed to take. Scaring others by sharing what could be no
more than ghost stories, wasn't going to do anyone any good.

"Just ignore them," I told her, to which Darius grunted in
agreement.

"I don't see what the big fuss is," he said. When both of us
stared at him, our palms illuminated with a comforting soft,
yellow light to help guide the way, he shrugged. "I mean, yeah,
it's cold—"

"The influence of dark, horrible magic," I reminded him.
Another shrug.

"So far, I don't see anything to write home about."

We'd been walking for the better part of two hours. The
ground we had covered in that time could have been accom-
plished in forty minutes outside of Hallowed Forest, but in here,
it was a whole 'nother ball game.

The canopy was made up entirely of dead leaves threaded so tightly together that barely any sunlight seeped through, despite the fact it was the middle of summer. The usual rustle of forest wildlife was gone, save for the occasional hooting of a haggard sounding owl—or the crunch of something large stepping on the crackly underbrush. We all whirled around every time we heard it, all fae present shining their illuminated hands in the direction of the sound. Each time, we found nothing.

It was a cold, dead, haunted place. Every step felt like we were moving one foot closer to disaster. We'd had to change course twice, navigating around stinking swamps that bubbled and fog-ridden bogs that sucked boots off people's feet. At this point, I probably couldn't find my way back to where we had first entered the woods even if I tried. Disorienting was an understatement.

We were all on edge. Gasps, cries, and muffled shrieks were not unusual sounds coming from our militia, which Darius thought was absurd. We were all magic-wielding individuals capable of fighting off whatever was thrown at us, in theory.

But who wanted to fight ghosts and malevolent spirits?

No one. I wasn't even sure I'd even know how, honestly. Theoretically, wouldn't spells whizz right through them? Whatever the case may be, at no point in Hallowed Forest, did I want to find out.

Unfortunately, the hairs standing up on the back of my neck suggested I might have to roll up my sleeves and give it a go. For the last, oh, fifteen minutes or so, I'd felt someone staring right through my back. That eerie sense of being watched had haunted me from the second I set foot in the forest, but now the fear had ramped up a notch—someone was *definitely* out there.

Keeping one illuminated palm raised, I stole a peek over my shoulder. Darkness and deformed, twisted trees stared back. The feeling, however, of two holes burning into me from behind, wouldn't go away. It only got worse. At the sound of something cracking, I whirled around and expelled a panic-induced hex.

The flash of green slammed into a tree, burning a hole straight through it.

The whole forest seemed to groan in response, a blast of frigid wind rushed over us, first from the left, then the right—like the charge of an unseen cavalry cutting down the enemy.

"Hey, keep it together," Darius snapped. Although he was facing me, I noted the way his gaze darted around, as if checking things out for himself before getting too far into his lecture. When nothing presented itself, nothing but the creepy feeling of being watched, he pinned his glare back on me. "I am *not* fighting a bunch of pissed off trees, Kaye."

I withheld my snort. Like Ents would ever live in Hallowed Forest.

"Something is watching me," I hissed, slowly, as quietly as I could, so as to not alarm Catriona. "I can feel it."

"Yeah, well, apparently, the trees have eyes," he said, gesturing half-heartedly toward the three storytellers in front of us. "Just try to ignore it."

I huffed, wishing he'd just have my back like always. "Darius, can you, for two seconds, just try to—"

"Company halt!"

The argument stopped at the sound of Quell's order from the front, and we closed the gap between us. I wanted to hurry up to the fae captains to see what the problem was—this *was* my company, after all, and I should be issuing the order to halt—but I got my answer soon enough.

"Defensive formation," Galen ordered. "Movement in the trees!"

I shot Darius a *told you so* look with lips pursed, to which he rolled his eyes, apparently nonplussed by the fact that we were about to be attacked. As we tightened up the spaces, falling in line with other supernaturals in the militia, all our backs to each other, gazes turned outward to the forest, I finally heard it: the roar of a gargoyle. Frowning, I slowly looked up to the dead canopied nest obstructing our view of the sky, for that was where the sound was coming from. A few more roars answered, then the leaves rustled as if struck by a strong gust of wind.

They were tracking us through the forest. Flying overhead. Apparently, it wasn't enough that Abramelin's army forced us into this decrepit place, but now they were in pursuit to make sure something gobbled us up along the way. I squared my shoulders, jaw clenched, and briefly entertained the idea of shooting a few hexes up through the leaves. I might even hit something.

But then again, I'd probably pissed off the forest enough with that last hex. Out of the corner of my eye, something dark darted between the trees, and I beckoned a brighter illumination orb to my palms, trying to catch the creature in the light. Somewhere to my far left, a skittering of feet through the rough underbrush snagged my attention, and Catriona shot her bundle of illuminated white light out into the forest, guiding it with a crooked finger as a witch might use a wand. The orb managed to cast light on *something* humanoid-shaped. Whatever it was crept back behind the tree trunk, its fingers long and lithe.

"Do we attack?" Hellas, a dwarf who generally said nothing and acknowledged no one, demanded with a growl. He had an axe in hand, poised and ready. I shook my head and lifted a hand to both still and silence him.

"Wait..."

Darius hissed my name as I took a few steps toward the hiding creature. Anxiety prickled through me, as I felt the eyes of the troops on my back, and my hands hummed with unused magic as I crouched down and peered around the trunk. The creature shifted back—as if in fright.

"Hello," I whispered. To make my intentions clear, I surrounded myself with an aura of white magic, which would act as both a shield *and* a welcoming beacon to potential allies in equal measures. One had to prepare for both possibilities, after all. "I'm not going to hurt you..."

A hush descended over the group as we waited, watching, prepared to deflect should the creature pounce. Almost two full minutes later, my knees aching and legs quivering, a young nymph poked her head out from behind the trunk, eyes wide and a little watery. Her skin, a pastel purple, appeared pale and forlorn; the Hallowed Forest was no place for a blessed being like her. She ought to be in Alfheim, bathing in a spring and surrounded by a meadow of forever blooming flowers. Her hair, a darker, more royal purple, appeared both rats-nested *and* flat, if that was possible, as she slowly crawled out from behind her hiding place.

"Stand down," I called, easing back on my heels. "Friendly supernatural, er, present."

I lifted my illuminated palms, just as Catriona padded to my side. Together, we lit up a good twenty feet of woodlands, and my jaw dropped as more nymphs slowly, hesitantly, exposed themselves from their hiding places behind the trees. Among them were a few druids, their faces and torsos painted with teal war paint in the old Celtic fashion, along with a few elves and dryads. While most looked haggard, no one appeared hurt. A few even smiled. Besides a few spears crafted from tree branches, they appeared weaponless—though certainly not magicless. While the forest was cold, the feel of these creatures was like the first warm breeze of spring.

Refreshing and comforting.

Slowly, I stood, not wanting to frighten them away with any sudden movements. My fae captains flocked to my side, encouraging me to make first contact, to ask for supplies, to extend an invitation to fight. I felt as though I could breathe a little easier in Hallowed Forest for the first time all day.

"OH, THANK YOU, THAT LOOKS..." I SCHOOLED MY FEATURES when something slithered through my bowl of soup—something distinctly tadpole-shaped. The druid continued spooning more of the milky-gray broth into my second bowl, though this time only a few root vegetables bobbed to the surface. When he straightened up and offered a shy smile, I forced one back. "Smells delicious. Thank you."

I stepped out of line and away from the cooking fire, over which a black cauldron filled with bubbling dinner hung. Not only was there something *definitely* alive in there, but the smell made me think the cooks had thrown every spice known to man into the mix. A quick glance around the campsite told me that most of the militia were forcing it down, spoonful by painful spoonful. Some were better at hiding their horror than the others. Galen actually tossed his into the woods and opted for a loaf of elvish bread instead, chewy grains and all.

No one said a word, however, to our hosts. After all, the small band of nymphs, druids, and a few odd elves had pulled us from our wandering and guided us through the bulk of Hallowed Forest. When it became clear that most of us needed to rest, the small population hiding out from Abramelin's bloodlust threw together a makeshift campsite in ten minutes, one that looked like it had been running for months, and got to work on making us dinner. Questionable dinner, sure, but it would be rude to refuse a hot meal.

I grimaced when the black tadpole *thing* wriggled through one of the bowl's brothy innards again. Darius could have that one. He'd probably enjoy the extra protein.

I found my dragon seated at the far edge of the camp, near the shimmering white magic wards the fairies of the group had erected earlier. Sitting on a log, he appeared to be fiddling with some twigs and dead branches, tossing them at the ward every so often and smirking when they disintegrated.

We'd beefed up our white magic with a few more dangerous spells, but you could never be too cautious with Abramelin's men flying around. Thus far, none had dared to enter the Hallowed Forest, and while the whole place was creepy as hell, it acted as a great buffer between us and them. With the nymphs and druids as our guides, we'd make good time to the portal at first light tomorrow.

At the crunch of ground under my feet, Darius looked up, dropping whatever he was playing with and wiping his hands on his pants. Nearby, Catriona sat at the base of a tree with a gaggle of nymphs braiding her hair. They'd been obsessed with its bleached, yet all natural, white appearance, since we met them. Apparently, they had been itching to get their hands on it. Catriona and I exchanged a quick look as I passed, and when she didn't silently beg for my assistance, seeming perfectly content with all the attention, I kept on walking.

"What's this?" Darius asked as I settled beside him on the log. One-half was rotted, so I scooted closer than I wanted to in front of the troops—then realized no one was watching, or probably cared if Darius and I sat beside each other. Maybe if I crawled onto his lap, we would get some attention.

Not happening.

"Dinner," I told him, stuffing the bowl with the slithering thing into his hands. "Freshly made and local, straight from Hallowed Forest—"

"Is something moving in there?" He squinted and brought the bowl up to his face, then pulled it away with a grimace. "What the hell is that smell?"

"Herbs," I said innocently. "Just eat it."

He peered into my bowl, body brushing up against mine. I swallowed hard and tried not to take a big whiff of his natural scent, something I'd come to realize was better than any high-end cologne out there.

"Why isn't there anything moving in yours?"

"Lucked out, I guess."

"Kaye."

"Stop whining and just eat it."

"Switch bowls."

"No."

"*Kaye.*"

I brought mine to my lips, tasting oak immediately, like the nymphs had carved it while the stew was cooking, then slurped the broth down noisily. The taste... Well, it could be worse. Woodsy. Let's go with that. Darius exhaled noisily beside me, some blend of an annoyed sigh and a chuckle.

"You think I won't take it from you just because you put your mouth on it?"

"That's the plan," I told him with a grin.

"Pretty sure we've sucked face a few times already," he noted, picking through his broth with his fingers. I uttered an embarrassing squeak when he pulled a wriggling black thing out and tossed it against the ward. It shriveled up and disappeared in an instant. When I faced him again, he smirked at me triumphantly. "Face sucking means your mouth doesn't scare me anymore."

"Well, it should. You have no idea what I can do with this thing."

"Not gonna lie." He took a noisy slurp himself, then gave a hum of contentment—like he actually enjoyed it. "I'm pretty excited to see what else that mouth of yours can do."

THAT USUAL RUSH of desire prickled through me—the same thing that happened every time Darius said something even *mildly* suggestive. A few weeks ago, I would have been all over that. Hell, I knew we both remembered a time where I was trying to get that sweet ass of his into my bed. Things were different now. There were... *feelings* involved now, and somehow that made all his flirtations affect me like I was a pre-teen experiencing the attentions of the opposite sex for the first time.

"Ugh, don't be gross," was my very mature response, which earned me a snort from my dragon. I returned to my dinner with a silly grin, cheeks warmed with a not entirely, all that embarrassed, blush. When I spared a look in his direction, I found him studying me with a sexy little smirk of his own, and I made sure he saw when I rolled my eyes. "Stop it."

"Stop what?"

"You know what."

I stilled when he leaned down, mouth resting next to my ear, and whispered, "Tell me. In detail. I want to hear it."

Our lips ended up no more than a breath apart when I turned my face toward him, and I noted the flutter of his eyelashes as those stormy grays wandered from my lips to my eyes and back again. Then, somewhere on the other side of the camp, an explosion of group laughter forced me to look away again, and I went back to eating my herb-infested soup, unable to shake the tension between us.

"Oh, Kaye." Another noisy slurp. "So, disappointed in you."

He exhaled something crossed between a laugh and a grunt when I slapped his leg – hard. When he stretched it out and gave it a shake, I knew I'd succeeded.

"I always underestimate your strength."

"I'll take that as a compliment," I told him. We exchanged quick grins before going back to our dinners in a contented silence. When I finished, I set the wooden bowl aside, wondering if I'd ever be able to taste normal food again with all this herbal aftertaste floating around my palate, and then turned my gaze outward. Although the forest appeared nearly black, I found myself noticing the shapes of gnarled and twisted trees, the rise and fall of thorny underbrush. If I blocked out the rest of the camp, I could almost hear the soft screeching of bugs.

Darius cleared his throat, and out of the corner of my eye, I caught him stacking our bowls and setting them aside. "You okay?"

"Thinking," I told him. "I've noticed my senses are kind of... sensitive lately. And not the usual heightened, magical kind. I just... I feel things. I see things. I can hear them. Even here, in a forest that is basically a deprivation chamber."

He snorted. "Yeah, I see it all too. I think..." Darius paused, threading his hands together with a sigh. "I don't know how this will make you, you know, *feel*, but maybe your shifter side is starting to present itself."

I appreciated the sensitivity he took with the topic, considering the sometimes-terse relationship supernaturals had with shifters. It wasn't that I didn't want to be a shifter; I just wasn't sure how to handle that I had a whole separate half of my being that I had only just found out about.

"So, what, now that I know about it, it'll start showing up in my everyday life?"

"I just think you're more open to connecting with your shifter side," he remarked. "You know it's there now. Things that you couldn't explain before about yourself are suddenly starting to make sense."

I glanced up at him after he fell quiet for a second time, only to find him studying me again, his expression more unreadable than I would have liked.

"But it's nothing to be afraid of," Darius added softly. "Though, I'd understand if you were. Having a powerful beast living inside of you isn't exactly easy. Dragons are next level difficult."

"I guess it'd be easier if I were a squirrel shifter, or something," I managed, picking at a hangnail. "I mean, how dramatic can an inner squirrel persona be?"

Not that I was experiencing some inner beast—not during moments of peace, anyway. That little voice, the one that had always steered me right since childhood, had become louder in times of real danger, however.

"Come on." Darius bumped me with his elbow. "Nobody wants to be a squirrel shifter... Not even squirrel shifters. Don't ever wish you were a squirrel, Kaye."

I laughed, and then leaned into him. Without prompting, Darius wrapped an arm around my shoulders, his fingertips lazily caressing my arm.

"You're cute," I told him, snuggling in so that my head settled under his chin, a hand on his chest. The steady *thump-thump* of his heart, constant and sure, soothed away whatever worries had started to creep in.

"I *am* pretty adorable," Darius said after a few moments passed.

I managed to slap his other leg this time—charley horse city, population: Darius.

~

NOW THAT I HAD "PROVEN" MYSELF A CAPABLE LEADER—ALL because I didn't blast some poor nymph into sweet oblivion back in the woods—apparently, I was supposed to lead the group through the portals. Galen and Quell had wordlessly relegated themselves to the rear of the group during our hike from the overnight camp to the portal on the other side of Hallowed Forest. I wasn't sure how *not* using violence had earned me their respect, but Darius told me to just take it—and take it I would.

"We move quickly," I instructed the militia. "The skies might be clear now, but that might not be the case in a few minutes."

It only took the word of one scout watching this portal, a small hobbit-sized door carved into the trunk of a century-old yew tree, and we would have the full gargoyle-witch armada on us again. After saying farewell to the Hallowed Forest dwellers, a few of whom had joined our cause, I exchanged a quick look with Catriona, whose gaze told me she would be right behind me, and then nodded when Darius gave my hand a squeeze.

The yew stood well over a hundred feet tall—a beast among trees, as it was. Sunshine bore down on us, hot and unflinching, and the air was just as still out here as it had been in the haunted forest. Apparently today was going to be a merciless summer day; hopefully that wasn't the case in Wisconsin, where the portal was set to take us. Good ol' Wisconsin: home of the bear shifter clans and not much else.

Pushing the prickly, stubby branches of the yew aside, I found myself standing in front of the portal door. I took a deep breath and turned to my comrades, knowing what I had to do. "I need a dagger, something sharp."

It took only a second, and I was being offered all sorts of pointy objects, all of which would easily get the job done. I cringed when a dwarf lifted his hand to me in offering and I saw that he was holding an axe.

Take it easy there, buddy. I need to offer a drop of blood, not my entire hand.

I accepted a dagger from one of the elves, used the tip to quickly prick my finger and offered a droplet of blood on the portal door. I pushed against the massive trunk when the bark darkened, beckoning me through. Portals that didn't take you to Alfheim were a little less disorienting; traveling a rainbow pathway over a bottomless pit turned your whole world upside-down. Local portals, ones that radiated a lesser magic than those that took us to an entirely separate world, were a quick in-and-out procedure.

Sure, there was *some* rainbow, but I could see the bright light at the end of the way, like rushing through a tunnel that cut through the underbelly of a mountain. Not wanting to occupy the portal for too long, I jogged through, only to catch my foot on something unseen and face-planted through the wall of light.

"Ooof!" I grunted on impact, hands slamming down onto lush, spongy grass. Grateful I hadn't totally face-planted, I blinked hard and breathed in the scent of wet grass; it must have just rained. My head spun, though only enough to be an annoyance: a few more blinks and the sensation disappeared.

Slowly, I lifted my head—and found myself staring directly into the face of a full grown black bear. Large, almost entirely black, eyes stared back at me, then widened into dish saucers when I let out a full-blown, unnecessarily, terrified scream and scrambled away, the heels of my boots kicking up grass as I went. To anyone watching, it would have been quite the scene, because the bear uttered something like a scream too and went bounding away in the opposite direction.

"Kaye!" Seconds later, my dragon came racing out of the portal, eyes dark and fists up. He practically exploded out of that little space, on the offense and charging forward.

"Over here," I said meekly, pleased that Darius and that fucking bear—a shifter, which I could detect now that I'd stopped being a panicky baby—were the only ones to see me act like an idiot. "I'm okay."

Halfway across the clearing, the beefy black bear shifted into a full-grown man—a familiar full-grown man at that.

"Colton!"

"Darius!"

"Embarrassing," I muttered to myself, wiping my grass-stained knees off as the two guys headed toward one another for the manliest handshake I'd ever seen. Colton, along with his friend Liam, had been the two bears working security when we visited the mage, Noris, back in Vermont. Apparently, the guys got around.

As more of our militia trickled out of the portal, one right after the other, all a little turned around on arrival, I made my way over to the two shifters—as usual, trying to be respectful of all the nudity.

Because... Colton had a *physique*. Meathead Central, sure, but I could think of many women—and men—in present company who would find him very appealing.

"Sorry about that. Didn't mean to scare you," Colton said, chuckling as I approached. Darius wore an identical smirk, obviously amused with my predicament, and it grew into a teasing grin when I scowled up at him.

"Yeah, thanks for waiting a foot away from the portal," I fired back, though I tried to keep my tone light as I shifted my focus to Colton—face area only. "You scared the shit out of me."

"Well, that scream could wake the dead, so I think we're even."

Teasing aside, we offered each other the usual polite greetings, his exuberance reserved mostly for Darius. Then he watched as the rest of the militia spilled out into the steadily, filling clearing.

"You bringing a lot of people with you?" Colton asked. Clearly, he had been alerted to our arrival, but I couldn't be sure by who. Zayne? One of my rebellious captains?

"There's a lot of us, yeah," Darius replied, and I bit back a smile when he referred to the other supernaturals as *us*, like we were all on the same team. Because we were, of course, but it would be difficult for steadfast shifters to accept working with supernaturals.

"Well, good..." Colton squared his shoulders, his expression the most serious I'd seen yet. "Because there are a lot of bears who need convincing that shit is going to hit the fan."

Darius and I exchanged looks.

"That," I said, "we can definitely do."

Okay, so convincing a whole clan of bear shifters to get on board with Zayne's plans proved to be a little harder than we anticipated. Years of anti-shifter sentiment within the supernatural community had left them wary of us, and Abramelin's crusade only made things worse. Fortunately for us, Colton and Liam had already briefed the clan on Abramelin's destruction, which made it easier for Galen, Quell, and myself to explain our plan of attack.

Having a shifter on our team helped too, though not as much as I'd hoped. The bears were almost as wary of Darius as they were of us. He'd explained that dragons tended to separate themselves, even from other shifter clans. As creatures of ancient lore, dragon shifters considered themselves loftier than the regular old, modern day bear, wolf, eagle—the works— shifters. It was a detail Darius had neglected to tell us, that dragons were the snobs of the shifter community.

Still, it had been very apparent that the bears were more willing to listen to him, and my dragon's established friendship with Liam and Colton, betas in the power hierarchy and only one step down from their alpha, went a long way.

All things considered, our first shifter clan was kind of a soft sell. Colton and Liam had coordinated with their alpha to mobilize the clan. We spent two days helping those who were leaving for a secret colony in Maine, assisting with the packing and planning and wrangling of wild cubs. Those who stayed behind prepared for battle, which, for shifters, consisted mostly of polishing weapons, weightlifting, and strategizing team plays against the enemy.

Like a giant, bear football team, only the big, playoff game would be a matter of life and death.

We did what we could to help the bears. Fairies created protection wards around the clan's forest community. Full of log cabins, parks for the cubs, and even a general store, it was something I could understand that they would want to keep safe. Our witches and mages created strengthening potions, protection charms—which Catriona and I planted just about everywhere—and even hex sacs: bags filled with magical ingredients that when they hit the enemy, they would explode and hex them. Boils. Unconsciousness. Blindness. Nasty stuff. Although still iffy with magic, most of the bears had been impressed with those in particular—magical hand grenades, they'd called them.

On the evening of our second day, Darius, myself, Colton, and Liam left the hubbub of the clan behind. The dynamic duo, who I had come to enjoy, led us out to the river, where the bears fished, almost like actual bears, most days. I'd never eaten so much fish in my life. Beers in hand, the four of us sat on the edge of a sturdy wooden dock, feet in the water, and watched the sun slowly set across the gorgeous blue sky. As we talked about everything, *but* the impending war with Abramelin, pinks, oranges, and reds colored the sky; our own personal television screen provided by Mother Nature herself.

With the rush of the river creating a gentle up and down bob of the dock, paired with a warm breeze that made me sleepy, this had been the most relaxed I'd felt in... Well, a long time. The good feelings aside, I couldn't shake a niggling thought, one that my new, rather loud inner voice refused to ignore.

"Hey, guys," I said, twisting around, one leg still hanging over the edge of the dock, toes lazily grazing the water, while the other leg folded up toward my chest. Colton and Liam were in the midst of gathering their empties before they headed back to the bear community, an easy ten-minute walk away.

"What's up, hybrid?" Liam grinned down at me when my cheeks flushed. Darius and I had shared my heritage with the pair earlier, while we sat here nursing beers and chatting about life. Colton and Liam had been thrilled at the news, though I wasn't thrilled with their new nickname.

"How did you know Abramelin was coming for you?" I asked, ignoring the desire to squash the nickname ASAP.

"Noris," Colton replied. "We were helping him clear out the village, and he told us everything. He said we needed to get our people up and moving or we'd lose them for good. Liam and I came straight to the clan and told our alpha everything."

Bernard, a black bear shifter who positively radiated the competent and strong leadership necessary of an alpha, already had a few scouts headed for other bear clans in the area to spread the word, which saved us a bit of time.

"Huh." Darius took a swig of his beer, the liquid sloshing around in the dark brown bottle. "Crazy ol' Noris. Glad, he didn't leave you in the dark."

"Us too." Colton gave a quick wave and a smile before heading back to the woods. Liam, meanwhile, lingered, his gaze wandering the horizon for a contemplative moment before fixing back on us.

"Even if he hadn't, we appreciate what you guys did here," he told us. "All of you. We had a plan to get everyone out, but you really sped things along. Cubs are going to be safe because of you." He shook his head. "I don't know how we'll ever repay you."

Darius held up his bottle. "More beer?"

"You got it, man."

I rolled my eyes. Trust a guy to ruin a sweet moment with a joke. After saying goodnight to both of us, Liam jogged after

Colton, who stood waiting for him at the tree-line. I watched as they jostled one another around, each swipe of their massive, meaty hands good natured, like brothers. Smiling, I faced the river and dipped my foot back in, wiggling my toes in the crisp, cool water. Darius sat beside me, our thighs touching, and appeared lost in thought, blowing on the mouth of his empty beer bottle every so often. Its soft bleating made me grin.

"So," I started, knowing we'd have to have this conversation at some point before we left tomorrow morning, "off to see the dragons next, huh?"

He offered a noncommittal grunt in response, followed by a curt, "Yeah."

"Your dragons, right?" I knew Darius belonged to the Sanctius clan, one of the largest colonies of dragon shifters in the country. A portal some fifty miles from the bear clan would take us into a mountain range, where we would find Darius's family. It hadn't been part of the plan that they would be among the first shifter clans we approached; Zayne made the schedule. With our departure steadily approaching, I'd noticed Darius getting quieter and more distant throughout the day.

"Yeah, my dragons. My family," he remarked as he started to pick the beer label off the bottle. "The whole lot of them."

I nibbled my lower lip, wanting to pull out more information, but not push him so far that he shut down.

"When did you last see them?"

"Before the curse," he said without missing a beat, like he had finally come to accept his past. "I haven't seen them since. I couldn't... You know why."

I nodded. We'd discussed the situation in some detail, though not as much as I would have liked. Darius's ex-girlfriend had cursed him when they broke up, taking his wings and his dignity. Unable to fly, Darius had left his family and struck out on his own, working as a bodyguard in New York. Him sacrificing himself for me the first time Abramelin's men had attacked the hive broke the curse, but we had been so busy with, the impending destruction of an entire group of peoples that he hadn't been able to go home.

Not until tomorrow.

"Do you want to tell me about them?" I asked. The psychologist in me wanted to poke and pry and wheedle out information until I had as accurate a picture as possible. After all, Darius and I were...*involved*. Tomorrow, I'd be meeting his family, his blood. Psychological interests aside, I felt I had a right to know at least *something* about his people.

Darius glanced at me, but continued to face the river. "Do I have to?"

"No. Not if you don't want to." Galen and Quell had briefed me on what the militia knew in general terms about the Sanctius clan: a large cluster of dragon shifters, an ancient line that went back to pre-America, and known for distancing themselves from humans, other shifters, and supernaturals in equal measures.

I couldn't fathom the scrutiny Darius may face when they learned he left them to go work for humans.

"I've got two younger brothers," he said after a few minutes of silence, nothing but the babbling river between us. "Quinn and Hayden. Quinn is the typical middle kid. Feels overlooked. Always looking for Dad's approval. Good guy, but ... I suspect he'll be standoffish."

My head bobbed up and down. "Okay."

"Then Hayden is a bit of a clown," Darius continued, and I noticed an immediate lightness in his tone, one that translated to a ghost of a smile on his face. "As the youngest, he doesn't have to worry about much. Just find a mate and give my mom some baby dragons. He'll charm the pants off you, if you let him."

"I'll be sure to wear a belt then." I laughed when he shot me a look, eyebrows raised. "Actually, I'll have to keep Catriona away from him. She's putty in the hands of anyone who can schmooze."

"He's a good kid." Darius rolled his shoulders back, like a

weight had suddenly been lifted. "Kind. Funny. He's never had any responsibilities, and it shows."

"And that makes you the brooding older brother?" I asked, my smile faltering when I realized what, technically, that meant for him. "And your dad is alpha, right? So..."

"Yeah."

"That makes you next in line?" When we first met Colton and Liam, they had made passing comments about Darius's role in his clan, about him being the next alpha, but with all the craziness that had been happening at the time, I shoved that revelation down and forgot about it until things settled. Well, nothing had truly settled, but after learning more about the Sanctius clan, I now had an inkling that Darius was more vital to his community than he let on.

"Technically," he muttered, scratching at his facial scruff with a sigh. "I'm the eldest, but you don't have to be the oldest in line to be made alpha. They've all known from the day I was born that I would be, though. All those eyes on me. Watching me. Monitoring me. Making sure I'm ready. So, yeah, I guess I'm next in line when my dad passes."

"Not to sound crass, but..." I faced him, noting the furrow in his brow and the stormy darkness in his eyes. "How old is your dad?"

"Old." Darius shook his head. "Old enough that I should have been there."

"Well, there were extenuating circumstances," I offered, knowing he felt guilty enough for both losing his wings and hiding away because of it. "And you'll be there tomorrow. You have the chance to make things right."

He stilled when I placed my hand on his shoulder, then, much to my surprise, leaned into my touch—to the point where suddenly he was resting against my shoulder. With no one around, I used the moment to stroke his hair, his back, his cheek. Slowly, his eyes drifted shut, and I vowed to do whatever

I could, to make tomorrow as smooth and seamless for him, as possible.

Darius had been my rock when my life took a turn for the dangerous. He had fought for me before I even realized I needed help. Tomorrow, as I led the militia to the Sanctius dragon clan, it was time for me to return the favor.

6

"Are you sure you want to do this?" Darius asked, his words gruff and quiet—yet somehow, they seemed to carry on the wind swirling around the vast stone hall embedded in the mountainside.

"It's not like I have much of a choice," I told him. "They asked for you and the leader. I'm the leader here."

A reluctant one thrust into the role, sure, but if dragons were all about tradition and brotherhood and some ancient, archaic code, then speaking to the sister of the fae leading this rebellion, was probably the best course of action.

"I can go alone," Darius offered.

"Do you want to?"

"Not really."

We stood alone on the top of an uneven stone stairwell carved into the side of the mountain. If Colton and Liam's bear clan had made me think of camping and cottages and sweet, humble dwellings, the Sanctius dragon clan took me straight out of the United States, straight out of the human world, and carried me straight into a sweeping, epic fantasy.

The community was built completely in line with the mountains, and two escorts had been waiting for us at the portal when we arrived early that morning. Unfortunately, most of us couldn't fly, and neither dragon offered a ride on their backs, so we'd had to trek through the rough terrain, far from any human contact and up into a mountain range I'd never heard of before. Great stone houses, halls in the old Scandinavian tradition, sat nestled amidst the slate gray backdrop of the mountain range, scattered at varying heights, but all situated along a winding road dotted with evergreens and fir trees.

As we arrived, Darius had explained to me, Quell, and Galen that the higher the house on the mountain, the more important the occupants. Naturally, his family's ancestral home sat almost at the peak.

Although shifters weren't capable of casting magic, to me the whole place reeked of it, and I couldn't help but wonder if someone had gotten here before us.

Darius had been greeted like royalty. Shifters lined the steep streets, racing out of their homes to welcome him home. Some even bowed, which was a new experience for me. My dragon took it all in stride, but his nervousness, which presented itself in the form of annoyance and a short temper, played out when a shifter dressed better than the rest, with gold trimmings, informed us that the militia could go no further until the alpha approved their presence in the village.

So here we were, at the top of a mountain, before the largest hall in the Sanctius clan, both of us hesitant about reaching for the huge brass knob.

"I... I could just go in by myself," I told him, forcing the offer. "You know, test the waters."

"I'd never let you do that."

"Then how are you feeling? We can take all the time you need."

"Kaye, stop analyzing me."

"I'm not—"

"It's pretty obvious—"

"Darius, I'm really *not*. I'm just being empathetic to your feelings—"

Both of us fell silent as the wooden door opened a crack.

"Maybe," a man's voice said, "you could stop coddling his damn feelings and just tell him to grow a pair."

Much to my surprise, the creases and lines etched across Darius's face disappeared, and he yanked the door open, revealing a slightly shorter, slightly leaner, younger, version of himself, right down to the stormy gray eyes.

"Hayden, you little shit."

"Hiya, big brother," the shifter said, laughing as Darius grabbed him by the shirt and dragged him into a hug. "Can't say I've missed that ugly mug of yours."

"Shut up," Darius muttered as they held one another tightly —just as Zayne and I had a month earlier. I stepped back, trying not to detract from the moment, but I couldn't help noting the way Hayden's face changed in the arms of his older brother. It had been grinning at first, impish and youthful, but the longer they hugged, the more the playfulness faded. Pain, fear, worry— they all flashed across his features one right after the other, until Hayden finally turned his head and buried it against Darius's neck. I swallowed hard, the unsaid emotion of the reunion catching my breath Looking out toward the village at the base of the stairwell, I blinked away a sudden rush of tears.

"Why don't you come in, ya lug," Hayden insisted, voice taking on a bit of an accent, a blend of several, as Darius patted his cheek. The shifter then turned his attention to me, and I shook his hand when he offered it.

"Kaye Allister," I told him. "I'm leading the militia in my brother's absence. I've come to—"

"Meet the folks?" Hayden asked, the impish quality back as he looked between me and Darius. When his older brother swatted at him, he chuckled and jumped back, all nimble and graceful where Darius was all muscle and hardness. "Oh, come on. It was like listening to an old married couple bicker out here.

You'll have to do better than that, if you don't want Mom and Dad to guess what's going on."

"I, er..." I deferred to Darius, lost, but my dragon just exhaled deeply and rolled his eyes.

"Hayden—"

"Look, get in there," the younger dragon urged with a nod toward the door. "Everyone's waiting. No one's upset. Well. Dad's a bit pissed. Okay, more than a bit." He then wiggled his eyebrows at me, grinning. "But Mom's the scary one, anyway, so you're basically in the clear."

I was ready to go in. Well, not *ready*, but feeling as prepared as I'd ever be. Just because Hayden figured it out, didn't mean his parents would, and technically I was just here to plead our case and help some shifters. Darius was the one who had something to be worried about. So, I waited, my gaze on him, yearning to clasp his hand but holding back. He had to make the decision without my gentle prodding.

Finally, he shook his head and strode forth, leaving both Hayden and I behind as he breached the hall, throwing open the door on the way. He walked confidently, sure of himself, but I knew inside he was feeling less than. Hayden and I exchanged quick looks, him grinning and me frowning, before he bowed low and gestured for me to enter.

I kind of liked the kid.

Shoulders back, I hurried after Darius, only to slow at the sight before me: Darius in the arms of a weeping woman—his mother, I assumed. While her hair was stark white, the rest of the dragon shifters present shared Darius's chestnut brown hair, although the man seated on a throne at the end of the stone hall wore a more weathered crown than the rest.

With Hayden by my side, I stopped a short distance away, giving Darius the time to reunite with his loved ones without me interfering. His mother coddled him as any mother might—or so I assumed, given I'd never had one—and fussed over his clothes, his facial scruff, and the length of his wild hair.

The older man, one who radiated power with nothing more than his gaze, remained seated, and I quickly deduced he was definitely Darius's father—and the clan's alpha. If I had to persuade anyone about the impending war with Abramelin, it was this man. While hunched, and wrinkled, each hand covered in rings and his cloak lined with fur like some old Viking Jarl, there was a sharpness in his regard, in the way he evaluated what unfolded before him.

And in the way, he assessed me.

I felt his stare long before I met it. Instead, I focused my attention on the family reunion. Darius and his mother were soon joined by another shifter—Quinn, if my family names were correct. Middle brother, he was less muscular than Hayden and Darius, and he wore his shoulder-length hair back in a ponytail. Of the three, he dressed most like his father, and carried himself like a medieval lord surveying his subjects. The façade faded slightly when he and Darius embraced, just as Hayden's goofy persona had momentarily dropped too.

All that fear. All that anxiety. I wouldn't say it was for nothing, but Darius was welcomed home like a conquering hero by everyone—save for his father. The man sat silently on the throne still, though I noticed his index finger had started to tap.

"Mom, I'd like you to meet someone..."

A rush of nerves prickled through me as the spotlight shifted from my dragon to me. Darius led the tall woman with stark, white hair over to me, her build athletic and wiry, and then, much to my surprise, he took my hand.

"This is Kaye. Her brother is leading the resistance against the Archmage Abramelin, and she—"

"Is your mate," the woman finished for him, her head tipped to one side as she appraised me. When I shot a somewhat panicky look to Darius, the woman chuckled. "My son's scent is all over you. And you... I feel a kinship with you."

"I'm half dragon," I blurted—as if wanting to please the mom of the guy I was dating.

Which, I guess, was basically the situation.

"Half fae," Darius finished for me. "And a fierce fighter."

I shrugged, cheeks hot. "Well, I mean…"

My words faded when his mom reached for me, taking a clump of my loose hair in hand and rubbing it between her fingers.

"Welcome to the Sanctius clan," she said. "My name is Cynthia. My husband, Khalon, has requested a private audience with you both."

"Mom, you don't have to leave," Darius muttered after casting a wary glance to the seated man. I smiled as she smiled, unable to help myself—I'd never seen an expression look so full of love before.

"Clan business first," she told him. "Then we shall celebrate as a whole family again."

Cynthia beckoned for Quinn and Hayden to follow, and the middle brother's eyes shot up and down my body as he stalked silently after her. The hairs on the back of my neck rose in response. Moments later, the large wooden doors at the end of the hall closed, blocking off the sunshine outside and leaving nothing but the flickering of a dozen or so torches to guide us forward.

"I feel like I'm in *Lord of the Rings*," I said under my breath, and Darius chuckled softly.

"Yeah, that's the general vibe of the place. Most of the shifters here are more modern than their ruling family." He spoke quietly and quickly as we approached Khalon, and while I could hear an attempt at nonchalance in his voice, I couldn't ignore the way he tensed more with each step. By the time we stopped at the foot of the three steps leading up to the alpha's throne, my dragon was a total ball of stress.

"Father." Darius dipped his head. "It is good to see you again. You look…"

"Decrepit," the alpha offered, lips curling into a snarl as he said it. "I am aware. I was wondering when you would show your face again to relieve me of this lifelong *post*."

"Circumstances kept me away," Darius admitted. "Circumstances I feel are better discussed in private."

Khalon's haunting gray eyes, colder and sterner than Darius's, flickered from his son to me, then back again. "Indeed."

"Father, may I introduce to you—"

"Kaye." The way he spat out my name made all the hairs on my arms stand up, like my name itself was supposed to insult me. "Sister of Zayne Allister, leader of the resistance forces against Abramelin's terror. I have heard of you."

"It's an honor to meet you," I said, stepping forward to situate myself between Darius and his father. No time for family tensions now, not when there were more pressing matters to discuss. "If you've heard of me, then I assume you know why I'm here."

"You and your brother are mobilizing shifter clans," Khalon mused, head cocked to one side, though his noticeable grimace suggested that the movement pained him. Every movement probably pained him. The man looked ancient. "He was once good, you know. Abramelin and I installed the defensive perimeter of the village in an age gone by. It was the only magic the clan would agree to. Now, I suspect it will lead to our doom."

"We can replace whatever wards he has constructed," I told him. "There are many capable fairies, witches, and mages in my group of resistance fighters who can create nearly impenetrable barriers. But we had hoped you would be willing to contribute warriors to the cause, too."

"And if I don't," he cleared his throat, the sound wet and gurgling, "does that mean you rescind your offer of protection?"

"Not in the slightest." I wanted to cross my arms, a meaningless method of blocking his unflinching stare. Something about it unnerved me. Maybe because the whites of his eyes had, at some point in the past, turned a sickly yellow. "We are here to protect, whether you join the cause or not. Abramelin has no right to spearhead a senseless genocide against shifters. This world, the one outside of human knowledge, is large enough that we can all live together in peace."

"Peace." Khalon scoffed, shifting about on the throne with more pained grimaces. "There will never be peace, not even among our own kind. Only a fool's peace. A false peace."

"Father, we haven't the luxury of time to debate your pessimistic philosophy of life," Darius said sharply. "Lives are at stake here."

"Lives that *you* will soon be responsible for," Khalon countered, fixing his narrowed look on Darius—suddenly I could breathe again, like a massive weight had been lifted off my chest.

"Father, now isn't the time to—"

"Lives," Khalon continued, followed by a long pause, as he coughed and sputtered. When the hacking died down, I swore I saw a hint of blood on the corners of his mouth, but he licked it away before I could confirm anything. "Lives that I am no longer strong enough to protect."

The whole vibe of the conversation shifted like the changing winds at sea, and I watched the air slowly leech out of the alpha's sail. It couldn't be easy to admit that he wasn't capable of looking after his own people anymore, people he had been responsible for over the last few decades. I spared a quick glance at Darius; while the tension hadn't eased out of his limbs yet, he appeared softer in his face, perhaps more receptive to what his father had to say.

"Abramelin is a dangerous enemy to have," Khalon said, his voice quieter now. "Not only is he an exceptionally powerful magic wielder, but he has much physical strength too, and a keen intellect that cannot be underestimated. He may employ the rabble of the supernatural community to do his bidding, but they are no more than pawns."

"Cannon fodder," I offered, and a sense of accomplishment prickled through me when Khalon nodded.

"Yes, cannon fodder indeed. Abramelin will sacrifice any

great number of his own men to ensure his goals are met." The old alpha's head drooped, as though the conversation exhausted him. His sickly, yellow gaze shifted to Darius. "You must lead our people into battle. You must assume some of your responsibilities *before* I pass from this world, as I cannot guide them in times of war. My dragon is old. He is tired. He prefers sleep to flight these days. I cannot bring him into the fray."

For a few beats, all we could hear was the gentle flicker of the torches. I held my breath, waiting on pins and needles for Darius's response, and when he finally gave one, it melted my heart. Slowly, almost carefully, he climbed the few steps separating him from his father, then knelt at the man's feet and took one weathered hand in both of his.

"What do you need from me?" he asked, the combative edginess sapped from his tone. His father sighed and placed his other hand on top of their clasped ones, and I schooled my features, so I wouldn't look *too* overwhelmed by the sweetness of the moment.

"Abramelin won't bother with the small clans," Khalon told us gruffly. "At least, not at first. He knows he'll need to eliminate the largest shifter clan first, *then* he can pick off whoever is left. We may not all see eye to eye, but the clans will rally together should one be targeted."

"Aren't you guys the largest clan?" I asked at that, without thinking. Both dragons looked back at me, and Darius shook his head, while his father simply stared like I was a moron.

"There's an even larger dragon clan," he said. "We're the oldest. They're the largest. The Brisbane clan—"

"Near Yellowstone," I added. "Right. That makes sense. Eliminate the strong and then squash the weak."

"What do you need me to do, Father?" Darius asked. "Tell me, and Kaye and I will see that it's done."

"Another time," Khalon murmured. "This... I'm tired."

Sensing it was my time to retreat, I told Darius I had to tell Galen and Quell we needed to change up our clan-visitation route—if only to give the two dragons a few moments of alone time to simply be with one another without anyone else watching. Darius had said, as the next alpha, he had been watched his whole life. Khalon was probably the only figure here who understood that. As I headed for the door to the hall, the alpha said that we were welcome with the Sanctius clan, to which I turned back and offered a bow, a gesture he seemed to appreciate.

And then I was gone, leaving Darius and his father to their hushed conversation and flickering torchlight, knowing in my heart that Darius had finally started on the path to his own private, personal redemption.

$\text{꧁}\quad 7 \quad \text{꧂}$

JUST BECAUSE DRAGONS were deemed the "snobs" of the shifter world, that did *not* mean they were strangers to bringing the house down with an epic party. After the militia had settled in various halls throughout the mountainside village, we were all invited to a feast to celebrate Darius's return. Considering all I had witnessed up to that point, I assumed the meal would be held in the alpha's home, with a high table and fur rugs and bards serenading us, as we observed some ridiculous form of ceremony.

That was not what I got—at all.

Sure, there was a bit of speech-making at the beginning of it all, but we weren't gathered in an archaic setting in the alpha's home. Instead, we were hosted in a more modern building halfway up the mountain range, with beautiful chandeliers overhead, and speakers embedded in every corner. The seating arrangement was more like a wedding reception than medieval feasting hall—and not a torch was in sight.

While the speeches made included the militia, welcoming us and thanking us for our assistance, I knew that most of the pomp and ceremony had to do with Darius returning.

And, why shouldn't it? He was their soon-to-be alpha. His father had to hobble around leaning heavily on his wife; he wasn't a man who could lead a clan of warrior shifters into a war against Abramelin. I wasn't sure what Darius and his father had talked about in my absence, nor had I had time to ask when we met up at the dinner. Quell, Galen, and I sat at one table, along with a handful of other supernaturals, while Darius sat with his family.

I hadn't minded, of course. Dinner had been exquisite: roast duck for each table and a myriad of fresh bread and vegetables. Chocolate made up the bulk of the dessert choices. The hall was cool yet cozy, and when mealtime ended, the real partying began. Unfortunately, when the tables were pushed back and the dancing started, I still didn't have much of a chance to talk with Darius. If his family wasn't chatting his ear off—totally acceptable, of course—then the rest of the clan was monopolizing him.

My newfound inner voice huffed and puffed for most of the evening. I hesitated to call her my inner dragon, but she *was* rather grumpy to be separated from Darius. Still, I did my best to have fun with everyone else. Given the nature of our being there, every day was *serious*. Lives hung in the balance. A madman wanted to kill all of us. So, just for a night, I didn't think any of us had a problem letting loose.

Catriona, least of all. My best friend had dragged a rather sullen looking Quinn onto the dance floor about an hour ago and hadn't let him leave. He still appeared miserable, but given that he hadn't stormed off yet, deep down, I suspected he was enjoying the attentions of a beautiful fae *way* more than he let on.

I, on the other hand, having drunk my fair share of specialty dragon wine, whatever that meant, had plopped down at our table and slipped out of my shoes, content to just watch at this point. The exuberant vibe rubbed off on me, and I watched the dancers with a smile, my gaze darting over to where Darius sat at a table with a bunch of other shifter men. He held a dark bottle of ale in his hand, his sleeves rolled up, and a grim expression tainted his features. He seemed to be doing more listening than talking. Every so often our eyes would meet, and his expression would lighten for just a moment or two, and that voice would just *sing* inside of me, thrilled at the connection.

It was nice.

I straightened up when someone placed a glass in front of me, then leaned back in my chair when Hayden settled into the seat beside me.

I pointed to the glass of suspiciously clear liquid. "What's this?"

"Water. Iron free, as big brother told us," he said, smirking. A faint sheen of sweat coated his face, like he'd only just escaped the dance floor himself. "You looked like you might need it."

"Thanks," I said, sarcasm seeping from my tone. "Glad to know I look like shit."

"Nah, you're beautiful," the dragon stated without missing a beat. "I'm just looking after my brother's girl. Making sure she's okay while everyone else talks him into the ground."

"You're sweet." I grabbed the glass and took one quick sip, then guzzled about half of it down when I realized it was cold and delicious. "But keep in mind, that your brother's girl is perfectly capable of taking care of herself, whether Darius is here or not."

"I kind of figured that," Hayden told me. He shrugged. "Maybe I wanted an excuse to talk to you."

"You never need that with me."

"Good to know."

As I nursed the rest of my water, we watched the dancers for a few moments. Without looking over, I heard Hayden shuffle closer, his elbows resting on the table beside mine.

"You know, I'm really happy Darius brought you home."

I tried not to look too touched, but his words made my chest tighten. "Thanks. It's been awesome meeting you guys—"

"I mean, it kind of clears the path for me," the young dragon remarked, grinning. "I've been dating a mage for the last six months, but I've been too scared to bring her 'round." He then nudged my arm. "You guys tested the waters and survived. Bodes well for me."

When he saw the look on my face, one I probably should have hidden better, he laughed.

"*And,* it's always nice to see someone make my brother happy," Hayden added with a wink. "Seriously. You're awesome, Kaye."

And with that, he was off, bouncing back to the dance floor and ruffling Quinn's hair along the way. I smiled, despite myself, and wondered if the whole point of the conversation had been about expressing some guy feelings that just *had* to be covered up by a joke. Whatever the case may be, I liked Hayden and wanted to get to know him better.

But for now, I needed more of that sweet, sweet water to combat the dragon wine churning in my stomach.

"KAYE!"

I slowed my mildly tipsy amble down the mountainside path at the sound of Darius's voice carrying across the night air. Gigantic street lamps lit the way, keeping the clan's village from succumbing to an otherwise pitch-black midnight. For some reason, even the stars were hard to spy out here, but I had a feeling that had something to do with Abramelin's protection spells he had cast over the village. Outsiders probably couldn't see the street lights either, but it was a terrible shame not to see the stars. So far from civilization, they must have been breathtaking out here.

When I spied my dragon jogging toward me, I stopped completely and waited for him to catch up, ignoring the way excitement bubbled in my stomach at his sudden appearance.

It was either excitement or the wine. I couldn't be sure yet. I'd been chugging water for the last hour, not wanting to wake tomorrow with a monster hangover, but it might have still been affecting me. Darius's cheeks looked positively flushed, his eyes a little unfocused as he thundered toward me—and, once he was close enough, he scooped me up with one arm and spun me around. I half giggled, half cried out in protest, hands pressed against his firm shoulders as my feet dangled over the ground.

"Where are you off to?" he demanded as he set me back down, yet he didn't remove his arm from around my waist. I cocked my head to one side, scrutinizing him.

"Are you drunk?"

"A little."

I licked my lips, trying not to laugh. "Well, I'm going to *bed*. There's a lot of work to do tomorrow, I'm sure."

"Father wants us to lead a parlay between the Sanctius clan and the Brisbane dragon clan," he blurted. I blinked up at him, surprised that he'd share the news with me now, but not entirely shocked at the news overall. I took a step back. Being pressed up against him... it did something to me. Physical contact made my head spin and my inner voice hungry; I found it whispering to caress his cheek, to brush the hair from his eyes—to kiss him.

"So... Yeah, I guess that means we'll have a lot to do," I said slowly, digesting the information.

"It's going to be all serious and dangerous," Darius told me, eyebrows twitching downward, "so you can't go to bed now. The sooner we sleep, the sooner it's tomorrow."

This time I laughed. "I don't think that's the way it works."

"One day closer to..." he continued, like he hadn't heard me, "I have to start... being..."

I bit the insides of my cheeks. The sooner he'd have to start acting like an alpha. Just because Darius had been raised his whole life to assume a certain role, didn't mean he'd be ready for it when the time came. His father wasn't in the ground yet, but there was a strong likelihood Darius would have to take over sooner than that anyway, given the circumstances.

"Okay." I grabbed his hand and squeezed, hoping the pressure would keep him from sinking too far into his dark thoughts. "What should we do instead?"

"Well..." He threaded his fingers through mine. "I know I've been a bit preoccupied with everything since we got here, so I think it's about time I gave you a proper tour of the place."

I agreed with a smile that hurt my cheeks, even though some of the clan's beta dragons had already shown Quell, Galen, Catriona, and me around earlier. They had touched on all the key structures to the clan's survival—the local school, market, blacksmith, tailor, grocery—but I had a feeling Darius's tour would have a more sentimental tone to it.

Or a drunk one. I couldn't tell; we didn't know each other well enough yet for me to know when he was piss drunk versus just feeling sorry for himself.

Hand in hand, we strolled through the village, sauntering down to the bottom-most house and working our way back up to the top. Darius stopped here and there, pointing out snippets of childhood memories to me with an easy smile and a warm tone, the kind that curled around my heart and wouldn't let go.

He showed me the clan bakery, where one of the shop girls had a crush on Hayden as a teen and used to sneak them all treacle tarts when the owner wasn't looking. We stopped at the school, where Darius pointed out the windows that never locked and were primed for mischievous brats to sneak in and out of when they wanted to cut class.

He showed me where he and his brothers had once played on dangerous cliffs as children, and the ledge his parents had thrown him off when he was first learning to fly in dragon form.

"It's like chucking your kids into the deep end of the pool, so they learn how to swim," he argued when I stared up at him, aghast.

"Only they won't plummet to a gruesome death, if they don't figure it out," I shot back. He shrugged.

"No. They'd just drown instead."

We toured the gardens on the other side of his family's hall, a surprising speck of pure, lush greenery, flowers, and herbs amidst all the varying shades of gray. He showed me where Hayden hid his very human motorbike, and the small cavern where Quinn liked to slip off to and sketch when he thought no one was watching.

By the time we reached the tallest peak of the range, standing side-by-side overlooking the village scattered down the face of the mountain and the valley below, I felt like I had known Darius all my life. As a gentle breeze kissed my cheeks and rustled my hair, I studied him while he peered up at the dark, slightly blurred sky, and it was like he had filled me with remembrance, nostalgia, and love. He made me feel at home with a lifetime of memories shared in just under an hour.

I'd never experienced anything like it before, and I was suddenly glad I hadn't gone to bed, as sore as my feet were and as heavy as my eyes felt. There was nothing in the world I'd trade for what we had just shared together—nothing.

"I see you watching me." His lips curved into a smirk, yet he didn't glance my way. "Creep."

"Shut up." I tried to take a good-natured swipe at him, but he caught my hand before impact and dragged me to him, capturing my lips in a white-hot kiss that I felt shoot straight down to my core. I inhaled sharply, rising onto my toes, as his arm snaked around my lower back and pulled me flush against him. I melted into him, my eyes fluttered shut, our lips parting to deepen the kiss.

His body, hard and familiar, had its own gravitational pull, pinning me to him. My inner voice sang at the contact, like the clouds had parted and the angel choir celebrated our union, and a sharp tingle of pleasure surged from the crest of my thighs when he bucked against me. Our eyes met again when we broke apart, breaths coming hard and fast, and I knew if I let myself, I could get lost in those storm clouds forever. Every inch of me burned at the slightest touch—yet the heat excited me, enticed me, had me desperate for more. More kissing. More touching.

More skin to skin—right here, right now, beneath a muddled sky and atop a range hidden from the world.

But I couldn't do it. Not like this. Not with both of us buzzed on dragon wine.

"Wait..." I angled my face away when he tried to claim my lips once more. His pressed to my cheek instead.

"Why?" he breathed, his grip around my waist as firm as ever. I shook my head and untangled my body from his, stumbling over the uneven surface as I put some distance between us. Darius's features darkened, and he crossed his arms, rejection hardening him. "You were all for this back at your apartment. Remember? What's changed now?"

"You mean back when you were an overprotective, annoyingly involved stranger?" I asked, eyebrows up. He stared at me, his cold demeanor fracturing within seconds, and we both chuckled. I shook my head and looked away. "Back when you were just a hot guy who seemed a bit intense and crazy, but could be a fun, little fling? Yeah. Of course, I was game then."

I could see him considering me for a moment in my peripheral, his expression softening. "Kaye..." He repeated my name gently until I looked at him, and he smirked. "Do you have a crush on me?"

I flipped him off, and he grabbed me before I could stalk away too far. Something about the way he held me felt different this time—no less electric, no less thrilling, but more comfortable.

"Feelings ruin everything," he muttered, then kissed my forehead. "But I get it. I've got a crush on you too."

"I just want it to be perfect," I told him, instantly regretting it. That made me sound like a virgin who was telling her high school beau they couldn't have sex at make-out point, or something. Darius didn't seem to notice. He just held me tighter, lips ghosting down my cheek and along my jaw.

"I understand." He exhaled sharply when I poked his stomach, then stole one last peck with a sigh. "Shall I escort you home then, milady?"

"Only if you stay," I told him. When he shot me a curious look, a suggestive smile tugging at his mouth, I added, "I sleep better beside you."

He snorted. "That's embarrassing."

"Oh, my god—"

"But I'm embarrassing, too," he insisted, holding me tight before I could slip away, "because I've never slept better in my life, than when I sleep next to you."

We shared one last kiss on the mountain peak, just as thunder rumbled somewhere in the distance. The summer storm hit by the time we reached his family's hall. We snuck into his childhood bedroom together, soaked to the bone, but happy, and fell asleep in one another's arms, eager for one night of peace before the real storm could sweep us away.

8

"Today you'll be meeting with the clan blacksmith, Hogar—"

"Hogar?" I snorted, despite the sour expression Quinn made at being talked over. "Are you serious?" A quick glance at Darius told me that, yes, his middle brother was very serious. "That's literally the most blacksmith-y name, I've ever heard in all my life. Did he apply to work here because of the village aesthetic, or—"

"Hogar is a highly regarded professional," Quinn said curtly. "He is the best at what he does, and is a master at forging dragon-specific armor and weaponry. He is critical to our survival, and should be treated with respect."

"Okay, okay," Darius muttered, clapping a large hand down on Quinn's shoulder and ducking down to add, "she was joking. Lighten up, little brother."

He then stepped around Quinn, who stood there with flushed cheeks and a pinched look on his face, and made his way toward the hall that doubled as both a blacksmith's workshop and, deeper into the heart of the mountain, the clan's armory. Catriona giggled beside me, as if amused by the whole ordeal. I hurried after Darius with my best friend at my heels.

A cowed Quinn followed behind, though I knew his mood

had less to do with the fact that I'd poked fun at Hogar's name and more to do with him being put down in front of Catriona. Since I'd had zero alone time with my closest friend, I hadn't been able to ask if she was aware that Quinn watched her like he wanted to carry her away and hoard her alongside a monstrous pile of treasures.

From the somewhat flirtatious sway in her narrow hips, I suspected that she *was* aware of the special attention the dragon shifter gave her—and liked it.

After Darius's father had instructed him to unite the Sanctius clan with the Brisbane dragon shifter clan, the largest in the country, and perhaps the continent, we had been scrambling to shift course and ensure we still had time to meet up with Zayne when all was said and done. While Galen and Quell hadn't been thrilled to learn we were now playing peacekeeper and unifier between the two clans, clans who had a history none of us were privy to yet, I had managed to persuade them, on my own, that this was for the best. If we could get two warrior clans of *dragons* on our side, we finally had an aerial squadron to combat Abramelin. Gargoyles would become less of an issue when huge winged beasts soared the skyways alongside them.

While many of the bears in Colton and Liam's clan, Ridgestone, were eager to do their part, they didn't strike me as true warriors. They were happy with their small, cottage-y existence, but their primal instinct to protect their kin worked in our favor. However, the Sanctius clan had a legitimate *armory* for freakin' *dragons*. Getting more of them on our side, united, ready to crush Abramelin's goons, was worth rerouting our whole schedule—the Brisbane clan had been last on our list of visits initially, as there were several clans scattered between here and there—totally and utterly worth it.

With the fae captains on board, which meant the rest of the militia was game, Darius and I had a day to get everyone ready to leave tomorrow morning. Just because this potential unification of the dragon clans was a good thing, didn't mean we had a lot of time to devote to it. We were still on a schedule, one that was now slightly tweaked to allow for a detour.

After following Darius inside the blacksmith's shop, I realized that not only did the man have the most blacksmith-y name ever, but he was the epitome of a blacksmith in physicality too: he rivaled Darius in height and had arms the size of tree trunks. His beard, though tied together with three hair elastics, was the thickest, most lustrous beard I'd ever seen—salt-and-peppered, black with shades of gray. Grizzled yet strong, it was clear that this was his life's calling.

"A pleasure to meet you," the shifter said after Darius had formally introduced us, yanking his thick gloves off and offering a hand to me. I took it, and he chuckled when my face lit up with surprise at how soft his hands were. "That's always the response. My wife's got a killer lotion." He then wiggled his bushy eyebrows at Catriona. "She'll kill me if I *don't* use it, o'course."

Catriona laughed. I noted how she gravitated toward Quinn when he appeared by her side—and he toward her, closing the space between them without a word, their bodies within a breath of touching. I refocused my attention on Hogar, who was still talking about his wife's demands, and tried to hide my frown.

But seriously, though. Quinn and Catriona had just met. Unless something major had happened between when I last saw them on the dance floor and now, I couldn't understand the connection.

"I'd like to take Kaye on a tour of the armory," Darius explained, "with your permission, of course."

"Hardly needed, lad," Hogar insisted, and I swore I saw him bow a little in Darius's direction.

"She's leader of the supernatural forces sent to mobilize us against our enemy—"

"That fucking Archmage, right?" Hogar spat in the direction of a great stone fireplace, the first feature visible upon entering his workshop. The rest—the benches and tables and tools and kilns and fire pits—carried on farther back into the surprisingly bright workshop. The walls were lined with axes, arrows, and swords; clearly, all were made by the hands of the scowling shifter in front of me. He looked like he wanted to do more than just spit at the mention of Abramelin. "My weaponry might not be magical, but I think it'll stand a strong chance against magic."

"There are many of us who can charm them to do more than just have a strong chance," I offered. "I'd like to take stock of everything, then send a few of our better spellcasters your way this afternoon, if that's all right?"

"Of course, of course," he said, gesturing toward the rear of the shop. "I'd be very interested to see what your lot can do to make improvements."

As Hogar led the way, I shot Darius an impressed look. Hogar was the exact reason you should never judge a book by its cover. He might be the epitome of some medieval blacksmith, all thick and muscular and hairy, but he seemed surprisingly open to outsiders sticking their noses in his business. I could think of many who would flip right out at the thought of someone tampering with what they crafted with their bare hands.

With a hand falling to the small of my back, Darius and I followed Hogar out of the shop. Catriona and Quinn brought up the rear. We moved from the illuminated workspace to a dingy mountain cavern in the time it took for us to pass through a single door. Humid, moist air filled my nostrils with each breath, and I had to blink hard a few times, resisting the urge to call upon my enhanced senses, in an effort to get used to the darkness.

Our march through the somewhat gloomy tunnel was brief, as it soon opened to an enormous underground hall—quite like the ones we had in the hive. Clearly, the clan had made good use of what nature had provided them, when they built their village within the magically concealed mountain range.

"Wow..." My voice echoed through the cave, and I could

practically feel Darius beaming at me. *And why shouldn't he be proud?* Before me, was the most comprehensive armory I'd ever seen, including the ones my brother had stocked within the hive. Weapons of all kinds, from dated swords to modern firepower, all had their place upon a blend of wooden and metal shelves. It reminded me of a library, although instead of running my fingers over the spines of books, I found them ghosting over blades, handles, and quivers loaded with feathered arrows.

"Did you make the guns too?" Catriona asked. We all ducked for cover when she lifted a pistol and pointed, one eye closed, in our general direction.

"Maybe don't..." Quinn hurried forward and gently pried it out of her hand. When she shot him a pout, he offered the most hapless, dopey smile I'd ever seen, in return. "You never know if it's loaded or not."

"Oh." Her cheeks colored as I shot her a *well, no duh, girl* kind of look. "Right."

"Most of the guns are imports," Hogar said, a slight edge to his tone. "I've built a few myself, but I specialize more so in the older, more classic weaponry." He pinned Catriona with a hard look. "And I ask that unless you know what you're doing, you don't touch."

Catriona made an X over her heart. "I promise to behave."

The wink she threw at Quinn did not go unmissed, nor did the smirk he shot back. I tried not to roll my eyes and made a note to grill her about all this flirting, later. It's not that she *couldn't* flirt, nor did I think I was the only one allowed to have a someone I could call my dragon, but Catriona told me every-thing. Feeling out of the loop wasn't a welcome change in our dynamic.

With the issue of refraining from touching what we didn't know sorted, Hogar led us on a tour of the armory. He showed us the blades he was particularly proud of, along with shields and projectile weapons that would help in the fight against Abramelin.

"My people can enchant the arrows to do more than just puncture," I said as I inspected the sharp, deadly tip of one Darius handed me.

"Arrows don't guarantee death," Darius agreed. "They hurt like a bitch and can possibly maim. Maybe the enemy will bleed out, but Kaye's forces can ensure maximum damage."

"Now, that I'd like to see," Hogar told me, grinning. I smiled back, and although I could appreciate his enthusiasm, the blood-thirsty gleam in his eye was a bit unnerving.

"Kaye, look!" Catriona snagged my hand as she rushed by, dragging me to the end of the aisle with a breathless smile on her lips. Just as I was about to ask what was up, I understood. The armory was endless, expanding into a museum-like setting with *dragon skulls* everywhere. A veritable dragon graveyard.

"Fallen warriors and heroes from centuries gone by," Darius said in my ear, making me jump. "Alphas from the past have been really obsessive about preserving history, so Hogar is charged with seeing to their care. I think he does a pretty fantastic job."

"They're..." My vision swam, and my chest tightened; the sight of these skulls, the sheer size of them all, stirred something within me I hadn't anticipated. Both haunting and inspiring, it was unlike anything I'd ever seen before in all my life—and very likely something I would never see again. If anything might encourage me to dig into my dragon roots, it was this.

Darius's hand curved around my waist, steering me toward him so he could press a kiss to my temple.

"Yeah. They are," Darius murmured. I nodded, pleased I didn't have to explain my reaction; something in the way he held me, the way he kissed me, the way his voice rumbled so sweetly in my ear—he understood without me having to say a word.

I could have stayed there forever, with Darius by my side. Maybe if we had time, I'd be able to come back and study each carefully preserved skull—to run my hands along the jagged edges of teeth, to examine the smooth bone, to feel as though I had a connection to these fallen heroes.

Unfortunately, Catriona's wandering attention span had the group moving again, and Darius and I reluctantly turned away from the graveyard to something I found equally interesting: two leather saddles.

"These are..." I bit back a laugh, not wanting to insult Hogar. "Huge."

"Well, you need 'em big if you want to ride a dragon," the blacksmith boomed from some distance away; clearly his shifter hearing was fine, despite his aged appearance. "Those are just prototypes, though. I'm still working on 'em."

His defensive tone wasn't lost on me, and I immediately wanted to put him at ease. "They're stunning, Hogar," I replied with a sincere smile. "Great job. I can't wait to see the final product."

"But do you *really* want people riding you? Isn't it a bit... insulting?" Catriona asked, her eyes wandering over the massive leather seat before chancing a feel. Her expression morphed from polite curiosity to a welcome surprise. "Oh, it's so soft."

"Only a dragon's mate has the honor of riding him, or her," Quinn explained. "It's hardly an insult then."

I watched him watch *her*, eyes blazing with an open affection, and then looked to Darius to see if he saw what I saw. By the furrow of his brow, I figured he had.

"Aren't most shifter mates fated, or whatever the term is?" I asked, to which both dragons around me nodded.

"Yeah, but that doesn't mean the person you're fated to be with must be a shifter too," Darius replied, his lips curving into a smile. "We don't choose who we're fated to be bound with, and every so often, shifters are paired with supernaturals."

"Our dragon forms scald anyone that's not a shifter," Quinn continued, "so Hogar is also working on protective gear that will keep you from burning yourself when you touch us." I noticed the bulge in his throat bob noticeably when our eyes met. Clearly Quinn would have no problem with Catriona climbing on his back and riding him.

"I'll never touch a dragon again," Catriona said quietly. "I learned my lesson the hard way."

"You've... touched a dragon?" There was that gulp again, some color tinging Quinn's cheeks. Darius and I exchanged amused looks before turning away in tandem, leaving the two to sort it out themselves.

"Only for a second, and it was just Darius," Catriona protested—a little too passionately, at that.

Yeah. We were *definitely* going to have a talk before the day was done. My bestie had some explaining to do—stat.

FOR THERE BEING TWENTY-FOUR HOURS IN A DAY, THERE never seemed to be enough time to do what I really wanted to do. When we finished with our tour of the armory, Darius and I had to go update Quell and Galen on all that we saw. Then, we needed to select the proper magic-wielders to go charm the weapons—those who wouldn't be thrown by Hogar's grizzled appearance were at top of the list. Quinn oversaw that, alongside Quell, while Galen and I worked with Darius to debrief the other dragon warriors who'd be traveling with us to the Brisbane clan tomorrow.

While I had faith in Darius's choices for the escort brigade, I secretly wanted to make sure there were no anti-supernatural opinions floating around that might jeopardize our mission. After all, just because the alpha family got along with the militia did not mean there wouldn't be rogue sentiments out there. Good people could still make bad decisions when their prejudices were preyed upon. In times as tense as these, I felt I'd had a right to worry that someone might snap at an off-handed comment—and barbecue a fae or two in the process.

However, after spending hours with the dragons Darius had chosen, I had faith that we had a good squad going with us. We were impressed with what they could do physically during sparring sessions with weaponry We admired their shooting skills down at the clan's range, and watched a few shift into the gorgeous creatures that dwelled within.

All that time spent doing those things ate into my day, until suddenly I went from discussing combat strategies to washing up for a slightly more formal dinner feast. This one was held in the alpha's hall, and it was *much* more ceremonial, with long tables aplenty to fit the entire clan together in the crowded space. Still, it seemed no Sanctius dragon was to be left out; they even had a kid's section at one end of a table, the dark wood covered with spills and dropped bits of dinner shortly after the feast began.

Unlike last night, however, when I was buried at a table far from Darius, something I must have done had warranted me a seat at the head table with the Alpha family. With the militia filling the lone long table in front of me, I sat between Darius and Hayden, with Darius on his father's right and his mother on the Alpha's left. Quinn sat beside her, and the seat next to him was filled by a cousin I'd only met when the feast started—Drew —and hadn't spoken to since.

Now, about a half-hour into the meal, Khalon rose, tapping his one long index nail against his glass. Within seconds, the hall fell silent—save for a few of my supernaturals, but I caught Quell shushing them with a glare.

"First," the aged alpha said, his voice surprisingly clear and steady as it carried over the entire hall—unassisted by magic, at that, "let me welcome you all to my family's home. As the head of this clan, there is no greater honor, no greater joy in my life, than to see you all here, happy and healthy, with good wine in your cups and delicious food in your bellies."

He pressed his wrinkled lips together as the clan erupted in cheers and applause, the loudest from the dragons on either side of me. I laughed, clapping right along with them, thrilled to see such an enthusiastic response from not just the clan, but from Darius too. Clearly, he and his father had used their alone time to settle some of their issues.

"Second," Khalon continued, and on the other side of him, I caught his wife Cynthia silencing everyone with a few gentle waves of her hand, like she was quieting a classroom of first graders, not a hall of dragon shifters. "We are most honored to be joined by our guests, the militia, led by half fae, half dragon —" More roars, which made my cheeks color profusely. I almost expected my militia to be surprised at the announcement, but then again, they had all sensed my heritage from the moment they met me. "—Kaye Allister. You all are welcome in this village, in this house, and in any house of any member of the Sanctius clan for as long as we all shall live. Your assistance in this conflict is most appreciated, and will not be forgotten."

We all raised our glasses and toasted one another. Like I'd known from the second I walked into the hall, something about tonight was different than the welcome home feast yesterday. There was ceremony here. Tradition. After seeing the dragon skulls today, I felt touched that I could take part in it.

As if sensing the faint twinge in my feelings, Darius's hand settled on my thigh. It didn't creep upward or caress inward. Instead, it just sat there, a comforting weight grounding me in the moment.

"Tomorrow, as some of you may or may not know by now, this talented group of supernaturals will accompany my son, Darius, your future alpha—" *More* cheers, no less earthshaking this time. "—on a mission to unite our warriors with those of the Brisbane dragon shifters, so that we may ensure the Archmage known as Abramelin does *not* annihilate our kind."

After all that we'd done today, we were ready to go. I, however, wasn't sure how I'd feel with dragons who *weren't* linked to Darius. Something about it made my stomach turn, both with delicious anticipation and pulse-pounding nerves.

"The journey will be perilous," Khalon stated as a hush fell over the hall once more, the crowd bewitched by the old man's words, "and I wish I could accompany you. Unfortunately, we all know that this old dragon is nearing the end of his days."

From the stricken looks on the faces in the crowd, it was obvious that despite his surly first impressions with me, Khalon was a beloved leader of this clan. I spared a quick glance at Darius; he had large shoes to fill, but I knew he could do it.

Not that it wouldn't be a lot of work, or anything. I wasn't that delusional.

My hand covered what it could of his on my thigh, and as his father spoke, our fingers knitted together.

"With that in mind, I want it known, so there will be no contention when Darius returns from this parlay with the Brisbane clan," Khalon set a weathered hand on his son's shoulder, "and he *will* return... Darius is my true heir. He is the sole alpha successor for the Sanctius clan, and whether I have passed from this life to the next when he comes back to us, the ceremony to elevate him to alpha will commence. The rites will be observed. He will bathe in the flame. He will be your alpha."

After such a proclamation, I honestly wasn't sure what to expect. Darius had tensed beside me, his fingertips now biting into my thigh, and Hayden had stopped fiddling with his cutlery to my left. There was no thunderous applause, no hooting from the peanut gallery in the far back. Only silence.

I swallowed hard, my heart suddenly hurting for Darius—until the first shifter stood. Another aged man, his skin sallow and his posture stooped, rose to his feet from the middle of the table to the far right. All eyes turned to him as he kissed his fingertips, then placed them over his heart, chin lifted in an almost reverent quiet that made my chest tighten.

Slowly, soundlessly, shifters around the room stood and repeated the gesture. Each time it happened, Darius's death grip on my leg lessened, until suddenly his hand was gone, resting on the table as he looked around the room. It might have been a trick of the light, the flickering flame of the candles at the edge of our table, but I swore there were tears in his eyes.

When the entire hall was on their feet—my supernaturals included, much to my continued surprise—Darius softly cleared his throat. His chair legs scraped the stone floor as he stood, mirroring the gesture with a kiss and a hand to his heart, eyes still shining.

My heart stuttered and confirmed what I hadn't fully admitted to myself. I *loved* him.

"There is no greater honor, no greater joy," Darius said, "and no greater fear—" The crowd chuckled. "—in all my life than to assume the position of alpha of this clan. You are my family. My brothers. Sisters. Aunts. Uncles. When this war is over, and we emerge victorious, there is nothing I look forward to more than coming home... at last."

Cue the positively *deafening* cheers. My hands clamped down over my ears as I laughed, then rose with the rest of the head table to toast to Darius, to Khalon, to our journey to clan Brisbane—and to victory.

However, it might unfold.

❦ *9* ❦

"OKAY, okay, let's everybody fan out... Give each other some space." I tried my best to issue the order without smiling or laughing or even hinting *at all* that I was enjoying the sight before me. In my brief experience with a dragon shifter clan, I'd learned a lot. Dragons were prideful, intelligent, and strong. They hailed from a tradition of warrior beings, and no one worried about getting their hands dirty.

So, imagine my surprise when almost *none* of those traveling with us to the Brisbane clan had ever used a portal before. Before we left Darius's childhood home earlier this morning, we had decided that we'd go straight to the Bighorn Mountain range in northern Wyoming, where the Brisbane clan had settled for the summer. According to Khalon, they had a winter settlement near Yellowstone Park, but this time of year, they headed to a more northern range, dwelling deep within, barricaded by magic and stone.

When I asked about the magic situation over there, I'd been pleased to learn Abramelin *hadn't* crafted their defenses, but rather they were more like the fae wards that kept humans from seeing what went on within the mountains. Perhaps a fae had done it—no one knew for sure.

Enter the portals. Luckily for us, there was one near the Sanctius clan—about a two-hour march—that took us within range of the Bighorn Mountains, exiting right into a secluded, wooded clearing. While all the supernaturals passed through fine, the dragons were having a rough time adjusting to magical transport. At least one had thrown up, many others complained of dizziness and difficulty clearing their vision.

"It'll subside," I assured them. "Just walk it off."

The group—about twenty dragons—were more inclined to listen to Darius and his brothers. Well, brother. Hayden bounced back pretty fast, being about ten years younger than most of the others, while Quinn sat near the portal, a hand pressed to his forehead, and wouldn't speak to anyone.

Anyone except Catriona, who I figured at this point had a bit of a crush on the guy. She had helped him find steady footing as soon as he stepped out of the portal, and had been by his side ever since, offering him small sips of water whenever his head popped up.

"Bunch of babies," Hayden said, chuckling. He stood beside me now, arms crossed. "It's no worse than a roller coaster."

I clamped down hard on the insides of my cheeks to keep from reacting to the glares a few of the dragons threw his way—if looks could kill, Hayden would already be six feet under.

We spent about an hour settling everyone down, although once most of the dragons started to feel better, myself and my fae captains moved on to other duties: checking supplies, sending out scouts, and mapping our progress. A dragon named Zander offered to fly ahead and let us know how many miles we needed to cover to reach the mountain entryway known only to the Sanctius clan. When he returned a half hour later, we learned that if we walked, it would take us about an hour and a half to get there, and that was if we moved at a good clip.

"It's doable," Darius insisted, countering the dubious looks shared amongst his dragons. "We have plenty of daylight left, and our supplies are good."

"I think some of you should fly ahead, to make sure the way is clear." This time I was the one catching the worried looks exchanged amongst the militia."

"Agreed." Quell crossed his arms beside me, Galen did the same on the other side, and for the first time, I felt like they had my back—and meant it.

Darius barked Quinn's name, and the shifter trudged forward.

"You'll lead the brigade in the sky," he instructed. "I'll stay on foot with the militia, and we'll meet at the door. At the first sign of trouble, turn back. We should be unified for whatever Abramelin might throw at us along the way."

"Don't you want to fly with us, Darius?"

"Yeah, come on, man, just—"

"This isn't up for discussion," my dragon said curtly. "You'll fly overhead, half of you leading the charge, half back with us. It's our best strategy so that neither group is singled out in the event of an attack."

A few of the dragons blanched at his tone, and while it might have sounded a little harsh, I knew exactly what he was doing. Darius needed them to see him as their soon-to-be alpha—not their friend. Their safety was in his hands, and from this point forward, it wasn't a democracy. I could learn a thing or two about leadership from him, but I was finally happy with my relationship with the militia and all its members.

I clapped my hands together, breaking the somewhat tense silence that followed. "Okay people... You heard him. Move on out."

Although a few dragons seemed like they wanted to argue some more, a pointed look from Darius and a few curt words from Hayden and Quinn got everyone moving again. Both brothers stepped in, regardless of how they felt, to have Darius's back—which only endeared them more to me, Quinn included.

During what would probably only be a few seconds of alone

time, I flicked Darius's arm, grinning when he glanced back at me. "Hey, thanks for staying down here with me. I'm sure it would be more fun to fly, but—"

"Like I would leave you by yourself in unfamiliar terrain," he said with a slight scoff. "Never. While the Brisbane clan will probably welcome *us*, they'll be on the lookout for supernaturals. I'm not risking it." He planted a quick kiss on my cheek, one of those blink-and-you'd-miss-it kind of kisses, and then met my gaze. "Or you."

I swallowed hard, ignoring the burn in my cheeks, and quickly changed the subject when I caught Quell and Galen studying me with concern.

"So, I think if I *do* ever fly, I should probably ride you," I started, and just as I was about to add *because you don't burn me and I won't need a saddle*, Darius dove right in and spoke over me.

"I'd love for you to ride me," he purred, a mischievous glint in his eye

The burn sharpened to a prickle across my cheeks. "You're so childish."

"You wound me." He touched a hand to his heart and pouted, then laughed when I shoved by him to go confer with my captains.

With the militia ready, supplies loaded onto backs and weapons half-loaded—just in case—Darius signaled for the dragons to take flight. Although I was sure no one wanted to watch a bunch of grown men and women strip down to nothing but their underwear, we all did, unable to tear our eyes away from the shifters as they transformed.

Dragons of all sizes soon filled the clearing, roaring into existence, the beat of their wings akin to a helicopter's whirring blades before take-off. I gripped Darius in the windstorm paired with the mild earthquake that followed the flight of twenty dragons, their scales rippling in the early afternoon sunshine. My dragon kept me steady with one arm—and held onto Catriona with the other. She laughed, shielding her face as dirt and loose forest debris shot up around us.

I wanted to protect my eyes, my face, from the onslaught, but I couldn't tear my gaze from the scene playing out before me. Darius had always been the most beautiful thing I'd ever seen in all my life, but watching all these dragons of different sizes, colors, wingspan, and protective outer spikes take flight... Well, it was easily a close second. Third, if you counted the skeleton graveyard back at the Sanctius clan.

Each new experience I had with dragon shifters was more meaningful, more exhilarating than the last, and for that I was grateful. As the wind died down and the militia collected themselves, I still found myself staring up at the flapping wings, wondering what it would be like to *fly*.

Would I be able to fly if I have the ability to shift? I blinked hard when the thought hit me like a freight train. I'd never considered it before. Despite my senses growing more acute, perhaps only because I was aware of the reason now, and that tenacious inner voice getting louder and more distinct, I hadn't even thought about shifting. I'd never had the urge to before, and even after I learned of my heritage, I assumed I didn't have the capability.

But if I could... Would I be able to fly?

It was a lifelong dream.

A desire I'd kept quiet since childhood, knowing that some fae lucked into wings, and others didn't.

"You okay?" Darius asked, his voice low in my ear. I nodded, realizing my eyes had started to water, and quickly swiped a hand under each.

"That was just..." I shook my head when I noticed the sympathetic twist of his lips. He knew. I didn't have to explain the impact that seeing multiple dragons take flight had on me. "I'm fine."

"I'd understand if you weren't."

Touched, I grabbed his hand and squeezed, knowing we

didn't have much time before the others looked to us to lead the way.

"I know." Another squeeze, as though our hands couldn't stand the thought of parting. "Thank you."

"Anytime, Kaye... my fae."

"REMIND ME AGAIN WHY WE ARE GOING THIS WAY?"

"It's a more direct route," I insisted, a strangled cry slipping out when my hair snagged on a pair of gnarled, spiny tree roots poking out from the cave wall—*again*. "Ouch!"

Catriona rushed to my aid, the bright white light emanating from her palms half-blinding me as she set to work freeing my red waves—which I should have worn tied back, honestly. We'd been in such a rush to get going once we arrived at the mountain entrance, one that opened *only* with a drop of dragon blood, the first magical door I'd encountered that deferred to dragons over supernaturals, that little things like wearing my hair off my face weren't exactly pressing issues.

By some stroke of sheer luck, we made it to the Bighorn Mountain range with no trouble from any of Abramelin's men. Our witches managed to conceal the dragon army so that any hiking humans wouldn't see them, and we had all arrived at the secret entrance known only to Darius and his brothers in a timely hour-fifteen. By then, the militia was exhausted, but we were losing daylight. The most direct route, apparently, was *through* the mountains, though Darius had told me they always flew over when they visited.

After a brief debate, the dragons opted to fly. One dragon, however, agreed to deliver a message to Zayne: meet us at the Brisbane clan. Time was slipping away, and I preferred we reconnect on schedule but in a different location rather than miss each other completely—and potentially risk an attack by Abramelin when we were still divided.

With most of the dragons in the air, we'd been left to travel on foot through the mountains via unfamiliar tunnels, with nothing but directions carved here and there on the wall in a script only Darius and his brothers seemed to know.

Apparently, we were on the right track, based on the vague directions on the walls, appearing at random. However, that didn't make the journey any more pleasant. As soon as we'd crossed the magically concealed doorway into the mountains, darkness encircled us—not a drop of sunlight to be found. Sure, the place *smelled* like the Hive, but in the Hive, we had a charmed ceiling that brought the outside sky in. Here, we had all our fae folk acting like giant flashlights as we moved slowly and steadily through the underground tunnels. Catriona and I took the lead at the front of the group, Darius and Quinn behind us, while Galen and Quell fell to the very back.

"You okay, Kaye?" Quinn asked.

"Fine," I insisted, wincing when Catriona ripped the last of my hair free. Mostly I wanted to get moving again; every incident that slowed us put us more behind schedule, whether it was someone tripping over an unseen boulder, or insisting they heard something skittering above.

"Catriona, are *you* okay?"

"She's fine," I said flatly, fighting the desire to roll my eyes as Quinn hurried to Catriona's side. He'd refused to join the others in the air this time, citing he wanted to make sure we got through the mountain paths okay. I, however, knew by now he just wanted to hold Catriona's hand if something jumped out at her in the dark, which I could appreciate. Sort of. "Let's go."

"Someone's grumpy underground," Darius teased, smoothing my ruffled hair down after sidling over to me. "We're making good time. Don't worry."

I shot him a narrowed look, then raised my illuminated hands and picked up the pace again. Telling me not to worry down here, with my entire militia behind me and no real escape route, was like telling an elf not to stop and obsess over a weed—not going to happen. There was plenty to worry about in such a small, cramped space, even with a band of talented supernaturals behind me, so I spent a lot of our initial march through the tunnels wondering if I should have pushed for Darius to fly over the mountain like the other dragons were.

No. I shook my head a little, more of a reminder to myself to trust my gut instinct. *We'd made the right decision.* My inner voice had even agreed with me, though she'd gone into a tense silence for the last fifteen minutes or so.

After what felt like hours of staring at the same dark, depressing landscape, the musty scent of closed in space lifted as we neared a cavernous opening. I enhanced every sense I had, focusing on piercing through the darkness as best I could and listening to the soft clicks emanating from the cave ahead.

"What is it?" Darius asked. "What do you feel?"

"Nothing," I admitted. My inner voice scoffed, murmuring in a low, whispery voice that I should trust my senses—something was afoot, even if I couldn't see it. I rolled my shoulders and tossed my head from side to side, as if working out a kink in my neck, and ignored her. "I just... I don't know."

We stopped the group at the mouth of the cave, then called all the fae present to the front. Together, we lifted our bright palms up, and even that couldn't entirely light up the huge space ahead. No sunshine still. Just a massive catacomb, whose ceiling I couldn't see, covered in cobwebs. No graves, yet a quick scan of the floor showed weak spots and holes.

"We'll need to travel in a line," Catriona noted with some concern. "Maybe three across?"

"And slowly," Galen agreed. "I don't like the look of this."

While the space appeared large enough for Darius and Quinn to shift and possibly act as ferries to get us all from one side to the other, I didn't like the look of the thick, gnarled roots hanging limply from somewhere above. They must have connected to dead trees on the mountainside; they didn't touch anything, just hung there. A few rustled, as if in a breeze, but I felt no wind on my cheeks.

"Stay alert," I ordered. "I'm not sure we're alone down here."

Those around me exchanged wary glances, while Darius exhaled a puff of smoke from his nostrils, his eyes darkening. Quinn mirrored his older brother's stance, moving closer to Catriona as my fae captains barked instructions back to the rest of the militia. I trusted them to bring up the rear again—though I wasn't sure I trusted myself to lead.

Not like I had a choice.

There was some debate over whether Catriona or Quinn should make up the third member in our front line, with Quinn insisting he be the one and Catriona arguing it would be better to have another magic-wielder at the helm. In the end, I made an executive decision to take Catriona, though I would have preferred she stay buried in the middle somewhere, out of harm's way.

With the militia organized and prepped, many with their weapons loaded or hands up, we descended fat stone steps leading down into the hollow. Like in the forests, underbrush snagged our pants and shoes, hindering our movements. Unlike in the forest, here it was cobwebs and dust, not prickle bushes and ivy.

We were halfway across the space, each step carefully thought out, when we spied a darker entrance straight ahead—like a door into another tunnel. However, as we pushed onward, I swore I heard something scuttle around to my right. I stopped with a hand up, shining my light in that direction. Nothing.

"What is it?" Darius murmured.

I hushed him softly, brow furrowed as I cranked up my sensitized hearing, only to jump when I heard the same scuttling to my left—coming from one of the black holes we were all trying to avoid. The hairs on the back of my neck shot up; no one else had made a sound. More scuttling, and this time Catriona's head whipped to the right in time with mine, her eyes wide and the light from her palm intensifying. Concentrating on the sound itself, I tried to place it, to give it a name. Not a clomping of boots on the stone. Not the slap of bare feet either. Something... less human.

"What are you—"

"Twelve o'clock!" Quell shouted from the back. My heart leaped into my throat as I cranked my head back—and swallowed a scream. There, dangling over the group, was the biggest fucking spider I had ever seen in my life. Like. Larger than an army tank, its eight legs like eight fuzzy sapling tree trunks.

"Hands up!" I cried, hoping that a blast of fae light might send the creature running. All the fae present turned as one, and the creature instantly recoiled, its plethora of eyes reflecting the light back at us.

"Arachne," Catriona said, voice wobbling a bit. "Descendants of the original... They said Athena turned a weaver into a spider for her pride—"

"Another time, Catriona," I told her sharply, then raised my voice to address the militia. "If it doesn't retreat, someone give it a reason to."

"Got it!" one of our witches acknowledged from somewhere in the middle. A few elves raised their loaded bows. The sight of that mammoth, hairy *thing* made my skin crawl, but I couldn't let the others see. Darius stood between Catriona and I, hands in fists, eyes on the enemy—unflinching and strong. That was what I had to embody too.

Just as I was about to issue the order—that spider wasn't crawling back up its web fast enough for my taste—something skittered behind me. Slowly, I turned back—and found another set of eight round, black eyes peering up at me, this time as an arachne climbed out of a nearby hole. A jet of green light shot out of my hand: a hex that would cut a target clear in half when used properly. The spider uttered a yowl when the curse hit, but its cry summoned more of its brethren to the surface.

A hell of a lot more. And it was at that moment I realized: these weren't frail old cobwebs sticking to our feet and slowing us down. They were spider webs.

We'd walked right into a nest.

"Kaye!" Darius's hands slammed down on my shoulders as the spider lunged out of the hole, and he dragged me out of the creature's reach just in time for me to feel the feathery soft caress of a hairy leg shoot by my face. Catriona toppled back into Quinn to avoid the creature, then blasted it with a pulse of white magic that sent it flying back from where it came. The sound it made—like nails screeching across a chalkboard—sent a shiver down my spine, the hairs on the back of my neck permanently up.

"Move forward!" I bellowed, taking off in a sprint across the hall, doing my best to avoid any potholes that opened into a black, spider-laden abyss below. While I'd expected the militia to rush after me, they just couldn't, not with at least a hundred arachnes of varying sizes surging out of every shadowy nook and cranny. All of them moving together sounded like one of those rustic rain sticks—like beads tumbling against one another as they fell from side to side, mirroring raindrops. Only these weren't raindrops. It was spider legs on webs and clacking pincers dripping with enough liquid to sedate an elephant. Within seconds the catacomb was filled with curses, hexes, spells, and arrows, the screams of frightened supernaturals bouncing off the walls.

"Stay together and *get to the other side!*" Galen screeched from the back—just before the enormous spider hanging over us nailed him with a spurt of webbing.

"Galen!" There were too many people between us for me to help, and I had spiders of my own to deal with, but I breathed easier—sort of—when Quell sprouted wings and sliced a silver blade through the webbing, freeing Galen before zooming up to combat the dangling arachnes head on.

Catriona and I soon found ourselves back to back, both of us alternating between shooting oncoming spiders, squealing with disgust whenever one got too close, and inching toward the other side of the hall. There were so many of them—too many, at least three for every supernatural here.

"Do you want me to shift?" Quinn shouted over the chaos. A neon yellow light—hex, most likely—whizzed by his ear courtesy of a nearby witch, who nailed a rearing spider in the belly. The creature folded in on itself and fell back into the webbing, twitching, bright white saliva foaming around its pincers.

"The cave's not big enough," I told him with a shake of my head.

"We risk hitting friend *and* foe with our flames in here," Darius added with a grunt, wrestling a smaller arachne onto its back, snapping a few legs in the process, before punting it into one of the gaping black holes. "Do *not* shift, no matter what your dragon says."

"Brother, I—"

"Protect Catriona," I ordered, knowing that would distract him. My best friend scoffed behind me.

"More like I'll protect *him*," she said a little snippily, blinding a spider with an illumination strobe that hurt even my eyes.

After using just about every curse in my arsenal, I shifted my focus away from repelling spiders—as many had fallen away, wounded—to getting the militia to the other side. My inner voice had been pushing that strategy since the arachnes first surfaced. She'd been getting louder the longer I ignored her.

"You start guiding them through," I hastily told Darius, trying not to shoot a glare up at my forehead—like that would do anything to silence the voice in my head. At least she sounded calm in there. Calmer than I felt, anyway. "Catriona and I will stay back and make sure everybody makes it." When he had that look, like he was about to argue, my eyes narrowed. "Darius, just do it!"

I inhaled sharply at the fierce kiss he stole before obeying, my body in overdrive—with fear, panic, desire. It wasn't sure which emotion to hone in on, but having Darius lead the others across the cave as best he could, certainly helped.

"Move!" I barked, gesturing for the battling supernaturals to follow my dragon. "We'll cover you!"

❧ 10 ☙

No one had to be told twice. As soon as they were given clearance to run, most of my supernaturals hightailed it across the hall, whether they could see or not, many of them moving at warped speeds. Most continued to fling hexes around the catacomb, while Catriona and I fought to hold back the onslaught of new, less damaged arachnes crawling out of their hidey-hole's.

A heads-up from the Brisbane clan that their mountain range had a giant spider problem would have been nice. I gritted my teeth, blasting one with a disorienting curse that sent it scrambling in the opposite direction. Just as Galen and Quell rushed by, with Quell in the air slicing at whatever was within reach of his daggers, a petrified scream sounded from behind me. I whirled around, heart slamming into my ribcage, and spotted Erik, a young fae who looked more wood sprite than fae, being dragged into one of the black holes, his body being steadily encased in webbing.

"Hang on!" I shouted. Then, without thinking, I leaped off our secure path, ignoring Catriona's protests, and bounced across the webbing on my tip-toes, trying not to stand in one place for too long, lest I get permanently stuck. A shadow raced by overhead as Quell zoomed toward the offending spider, and the beast screeched, that same nails-on-chalkboard sound, when one of the fae's silver blades embedded in its side. A few quick blasts of white magic from me broke the webbing around Erik, and I all but dragged him away from the edge of that black hole—trying not to dwell on the fact that more skittering, shuffling shapes were crawling toward me.

"Give me his hand," Quell ordered, and I pushed the wounded fae up to him, noting that the spider had sunk its fangs into him at some point. He'd be unconscious soon—but so would I if I didn't get the hell out of there. With a burst of fae speed, I made it back to the walkway and out of the deep webs in good time. Catriona stood waiting for me, all by herself, blasting spiders off left, right, and center. Her face screwed up in concentration, one that didn't lift even when I grabbed her arm and ran, one palm illuminated to guide the way.

"Run!"

"I'm trying!" she shouted back.

As we neared the exit, which seemed to have a light some-where nearby, the spiders swarmed us, closing in on all sides—and they would have taken us too, had it not been for Catriona's quick thinking. My foot snagged on some webbing as we crossed from catacomb to claustrophobic tunnel, sending me tumbling *and* dragging Catriona down after me. However, before we'd even hit the ground, Catriona sealed the opening with a very basic protection ward, her hands trembling. Spiders slammed into the shimmering surface—and bounced off, screeching their dismay, poison foaming down their fangs, and beady black eyes staring us down hungrily.

"Oh, my god," I whispered, letting my head fall back onto the ground. Adrenaline forced my body to shake, my head filled with fog, my inner voice finally quiet, as Catriona flopped down beside me.

"Tell me about it," she said, groaning. While I could hear the fading voices of our militia in the distance, for the moment, we were alone. I needed the quiet, the privacy, to recover. However, my peace was cut short by the sound of thundering footsteps clomping toward us, and as I sat up, I spied Darius and Quinn rounding the gentle curve of the tunnel, torches in hand.

"Catriona!" Quinn was on her in a second, hastily helping her to her feet. Darius, meanwhile, had stopped some five feet from me, relief washing over his features as I stood.

"You okay?" he asked, voice huskier, darker—strained, almost. "I hate that you made me leave you in there."

I caught it then, the barely suppressed rage mingled with fear. It made my eyes water.

"I'm fine," I told him, quickly brushing the tears away. "Thanks to Catriona, anyway. We're all good."

We stared at one another for a moment, until Darius closed the distance between us in a few hard steps and dragged me into his arms. I closed my eyes, squeezing tightly, allowing the feelings of a near-death experience—another to add to my collection, I supposed—to wash over me while no one else could see.

"Thanks for coming back for me," I murmured against his neck. I felt him swallow hard, his hand in my hair; the other arm wrapped so tightly around my waist that breathing became a chore.

"Always, Kaye. When are you going to get it through your head?" He let out a tense chuckle, and I realized at that moment that he was shaking too. "I'll *always* come back for you."

"ARE WE SURE THIS PLACE ISN'T IN A DIFFERENT REALM?" I gave the plump, purple, though ultimately unidentifiable, fruit in my hand an experimental squeeze. "I mean... Are we sure we're even on Earth anymore?"

"The Brisbane clan isn't afraid to use magic to enhance their lives," Darius said as he slowly paced back and forth between two trees out of dozens where these delicious purple fruits grew. We'd marked them safe about an hour ago, when we stumbled out of the seemingly endless underground mountain tunnels into a lush valley. So far, no snakes waited to damn us in this garden of Eden, but the day wasn't over yet. Rich, green grass stretched as far as the eye could see in a valley between two looming mountains. Overhead, the early evening summer sun cast a warm orange glow across the oasis. Not a spider in sight—but orchards of fruit-bearing trees, fields of sunflowers, and pools of clear blue water lay before us instead.

After all the time we'd spent inside the mountain, it had taken a lot of restraint not to dive headfirst into paradise. Our tangle with the spiders, however, had left all of us on edge, and we hunkered down near the small doorway along the mountain's face. We were definitely above sea-level, so I couldn't quite call it the mountain's base. There we tended to our wounded, replenished our fluids, and took time to reassess the situation. While we could see the sky overhead, there wasn't a dragon in sight, and we couldn't be sure if they'd surpassed us by now or not.

But if Darius's estimation was correct, and it took under two hours to reach the Brisbane clan stronghold by air, we were way behind.

The day wasn't over yet, however. We still had a chance to make up for lost time—as long as there wasn't a swarm of giant, killer bees waiting in the sunflower fields.

"Father says the clan employs a few supernaturals as a means to build up their defenses," Quinn added. He and Catriona sat beneath the shade of a tree, one that reminded me of cherry trees in full bloom, while the rest of the militia sat scattered around us, recovering. "This is supposed to be their summer retreat. It wouldn't surprise me, if they used magic to spruce the place up a bit. Mountain landscape loses its charm after a while."

"Well, you guys would know mountain living," I said, setting the fruit aside in favor of a few nibbles of fae bread from my pack. As they discussed the possibilities of this being magically-grown beauty, I let my gaze wander through the orchard, up to the leaves swaying in a gentle breeze. The movement was hypnotic, and with how exhausted my whole body felt, it would have been easy to lie back and sleep until next Sunday.

No sleeping. Not here.

I rolled onto my side and ignored the whispers in my head. If I didn't know I was a shifter I would think I was mentally disturbed. Fae didn't hear voices, even if it was just the one.

Before I could sink too far into my thoughts, a figure caught my attention. A face, poking out from behind a nearby tree—the face of a little girl. I frowned and pushed myself up onto my knees. She darted behind the trunk, then slowly looked out again. Grayish skin, sickly almost, paired with straggly long, black hair. When my emerald greens met her near black ones, she smiled, revealing two rows of yellowing teeth.

All things considered, she was rather frightening in appearance—yet I couldn't look away. At that moment, all I wanted was to protect her, to sweep her into my arms and soothe whatever might ail her.

"Kaye..." Darius sounded far away as I staggered to my feet, then lurched toward the girl, who giggled and darted deeper into the trees. He called my name again, his voice muffled and lost in the wind, and I took off with a burst of fae speed, not wanting to lose this precious little creature.

Slowly, Kaye. Slowly.

"Shut up," I snapped, pushing harder. Where could the girl have gone? She was *just* here. Panic gripped me, pulse-pounding *fear* that she was lost—until that giggle washed over me again, guiding me toward her. I let my feet do their thing, staggering through the orchard, narrowly avoiding trees and unearthed roots, until I finally found her. She stood at the edge of a small pool, her arms opened to me like she wanted a hug.

And I was desperate to comply. Relief flooded through me, the feeling better than the effect of any drug in this world or the next.

"Thank goodness," I breathed as I stumbled for her. "There you are!"

"Kaye!" Two hands clamped down hard on my shoulder, and I shrieked as someone dragged me away, while another knocked me onto my back. I blinked up in surprise to find Galen and Catriona standing over me. A quick glance back showed Darius racing toward us. I frowned.

What the hell was I doing here? Why was I on my back—and why did I feel as though I'd just been to hell and back? Everything hurt and what little energies I'd been rebuilding after our bout with the spiders were drained.

I set a hand on my forehead, the world spinning as Catriona helped me sit up. "W-What?"

"She's an Archeri," Galen told me. His hands pulsed with white magic, and when I looked back to that creature, that thing I'd thought was a little angel, I realized he was keeping her at bay. And she was screaming a soundless shriek; her jaw dropped open down to her chest, mouth full of razor-sharp teeth. Her hands looked more like claws now, and her dress had gone from Sunday School perfect to tattered and thin, a flash of emaciated ribcage catching my eye as she tried to get back to us.

"A demon who takes the form of a girl," Catriona added, shuffling back as Darius wrapped an arm around my waist and hauled me to my feet—and didn't let go.

"But she—"

"They bewitch their victims when you make eye contact," Catriona continued, darting behind Darius and peering over his shoulder. "Their goal is to make you sick. She feeds off you, then leaves you diseased and broken."

"*Bitch*," I spat, glowering at her. I didn't have the energy to fight, to be angry, to even try to tear her limb from limb. She'd stolen that from me with no more than a look.

"We should kill her," Galen insisted, his arms quivering as he kept her back. "And any others we might see."

"They tend to hunt alone," Catriona said. "They *do* usually live in the mountains though."

"I can rip her in half and be done with it," Darius growled.

He held me up, not back, my body sagging in his arms. "Let me—"

Before any of us could do *anything*, a scaly arm shot up from the water, breaking the surface with a huge splash. Talon-tipped fingers wrapped around the girl's ankle, then dragged her into the water as she shrieked. The surface rippled and bubbled for a few seconds, then went perfectly still as we stared in a stunned silence.

"This place is fucked," I muttered.

Darius tightened his hold on me. "Slightly."

"Let's get the hell out of here...now."

"*Agreed*," everyone else said in unison, and we hastily made our way back to the group, always looking over our shoulders, tensed and ready for the next attack of supernatural bullshit that this faux paradise had to offer.

❧   II   ☙

AS I WATCHED two sentries lead Darius away, a lead weight made itself at home in the pit of my stomach. Being separated from him, seeing him escorted by two armed men toward a gothic castle, embedded in the mountains, sent a flutter of pulsing anxiety through me. It made my palms clammy and my knees weak, but I just stood there, head held high, and watched him go. I couldn't let anyone see how this affected me. Not the militia. Not my captains. Not even Catriona. And definitely not the dozen or so armed shifters patrolling the outer wall of the castle, a barricade that stretched some fifty or sixty feet up. I'd no idea what kind of weapons they had up there, but the men who came to collect Darius had automatic assault rifles strapped to them like they were headed for human combat.

I wasn't sure what to make of that, and from the tight expressions on Galen and Quell's face, neither did they.

The two dragons escorted Darius to a metal gate, one that looked like it could withstand a battering ram, its foot-long iron spikes covering it from top to bottom making it far less inviting than that valley of greenery and danger. We had spent the last hour trekking through it, on high alert for more Archeri and whatever else these magical mountains held. Thankfully, there were no further monsters to battle, but we arrived at the gates of the Brisbane clan's castle exhausted. Drained. I could barely force my legs to move, but I pushed myself, hoping that I'd be granted access alongside Darius.

"No supernaturals yet," one of the sentries had barked at me, and that was that. We were to set up camp outside while Darius pleaded our case to the clan's alpha. While the Sanctius clan dragons were our shifter allies, there were more of us supernaturals than there were of them. They had been just as quick to argue with the armed escorts, demanding we at least wait *inside* the castle walls. After the Sanctius dragons had heard what we supernaturals had gone through to get there on foot, no one was keen on waiting in the barren, rocky mountain pass while Darius chatted up the alpha inside. Brisbane security was having none of it, so here we were—waiting.

Darius met my eye right before the gates swung closed. Although he said nothing to me, I sensed that he wanted me to stay strong. To watch the others. To not panic. He'd be back.

He would always come back for me.

I gave the slightest nod, hoping he saw it before the wrought iron doors slammed shut. Just being near them made me nauseous, and I instructed the militia's fae population to set up camp as far from the doors as possible. If we had to be out here for the night, there was no sense in weakening some of my best fighters in the process.

"What do we do now?" Galen whispered. He and Quell cornered me as the others started to set up camp, the rustle of pots and pans ever present with all the hungry bellies to feed.

"We wait," I told him. "That's all we can do."

Something moved in the corner of my eye, and a quick glance up to the looming mountains around us, told me that not only were there eyes watching us from the castle's walls, but there were dragon shifters situated all around us. Cloaked in gray, they perched on ledges, sizing us up, assessing our threat level, keeping a close eye on our activity.

"They're pretty damn fortified for this being a summer retreat," Galen noted, and I nodded.

"Khalon knew Abramelin was after them before we arrived." Quell sighed. "It wouldn't surprise me if the Brisbane clan had already started arming themselves for war too."

"Good," I said as I continued counting the shifter scouts semi-hidden across the mountain landscape. "I hope they give Abramelin hell..."

~

I JOLTED OUT OF MY LIGHT DOZING WHEN A HAND CLAMPED down on my shoulder, bolting upright and nailing whoever touched me, right in the nose.

"*Fuck*, Kaye," Darius groaned, falling back on his ass, hands over his nose, scowling at me. Heart racing, I scrambled across my temporary sleeping arrangements—a sleeping bag I'd enchanted to feel as downy and soft as my old mattress—and quickly worked on healing what I realized was a broken nose.

"Sorry," I whispered, infusing the break with white magic, willing the bones to mend. "It took me forever to get to sleep..."

My brain shifted into high gear, and I suddenly realized he was back. Out of the castle. In our camp. Unharmed! Well, besides the broken nose, now healed. "When did you get here?"

"Just now," he said, brushing my hands away, when I continued fussing over him. "I'm fine. I'm fine. I shouldn't have startled you."

"It's okay," I managed as we both climbed into my sleeping bag. It had been hours since I last saw Darius. We'd settled in for the night, with a few fires going and people watching the camp in shifts. I was supposed to be getting my much-needed sleep, but I'd been tossing and turning for at least an hour or two. I couldn't have been asleep for long before Darius roused me, and as much as I wanted to poke fun at him, to hug him, maybe risk a kiss, I knew as leader of this militia, I had more pressing priorities. "What happened in there? Did you meet the alpha? Are they going to help us? Can we go inside? What—"

"Whoa, whoa, whoa." He chuckled, calming me like a frightened animal. "Everything is fine. The alpha knew of Abramelin's plans and has been arming his people accordingly. He says we can come inside in the morning."

"Why not now?"

"He wants to tell the rest of the clan that we're here. They know they're in a war with supernaturals. The alpha wants to ease them into it, though he expressed his appreciation for our being here."

I tried not to glare at the castle and its barricade looming over our camp. "Huh."

"He's a good man. A warrior and a true alpha," Darius insisted. "He worries about his people, and unlike many dragon clans in the past, he wants to work *with* us rather than handling it on his own, in private. He's let the other clans set up camp on the other side of the castle too. They'll be allowed entry when we are."

My eyebrows shot up. "The other clans?"

"Bears. Wolves." He shrugged. "They've been arriving for a few days now, apparently. There's another entryway. I guess we arrived at the back door." He grinned like a little boy who'd been caught misbehaving when I frowned. "My bad. I thought I knew where I was going."

"More Sanctius dragons arrived while you were gone," I told him before I could forget. "They said they were out-of-towners, the guys who don't live with the clan. About thirty more."

"Excellent." He scanned the dark campsite. "I hope my brothers thanked them in my stead."

"I did," I said. "Hope that's good enough."

"Better than good enough", he replied. I exhaled sharply when he stole a kiss, his hand cupping my face. "Don't take this the wrong way Kaye, but you look exhausted. Go back to sleep. We'll talk about all this in the morning."

"But—"

"You're no good to anyone half-asleep. You'll need your wits about you to play in the Brisbane clan court. They run themselves like a medieval kingdom... Even more so than we do."

I blinked sleepily, fascinated, and tried to ask more, but Darius hushed me with more soft kisses and slowly eased me back down onto the sleeping bag. My heart fluttered, my hands were desperate to roam his body—but the rest of me was too tired to lift them.

"Sleep," he murmured against my lips, then pressed a kiss to my forehead. I managed to catch the hem of his t-shirt when he started to leave.

"Sleep with me," I pleaded softly. His storm-gray eyes darted around the camp again, but he soon settled down next to me. Within seconds, I'd burrowed against his burly chest, breathing him in, his scent soothing the inner pangs of longing that had grown sharper, more painful in his absence. Arms wrapped around me, he stroked my hair, and for the first time all night, sleep came easily.

~

I AWOKE TO THE SOUND OF GUNFIRE. GUNFIRE AND screaming.

At first, I'd thought it was part of my dream—because it would have fit right in. Shit had been hitting the fan for what felt like an eternity inside my head: war, strife, fire. Even in Darius's arms, I hadn't been able to escape the onslaught of nightmares.

I groaned, shielding my eyes from an unrelenting sun, and rolled onto my back.

"Get down!"

The voice that issued the order wasn't one of ours. My eyes shot open, and I instantly realized it wasn't the sun that was nearly blinding me, but a flaming ball of magical *something* hurtling toward camp like a falling star.

Even as panic sunk its icy claws into my heart, I still leaped to my feet, Darius was nowhere to be seen, and threw myself toward the nearest cluster of militia members. Just before impact, I cast a protective ward around the six of us—it was all I could muster in the heat of the moment—and braced for impact.

I had expected the magical canon ball to slam into the camp, butchering anyone who wasn't protected by a shield of some kind. Instead, it smashed into the enormous wall barring outsiders from the Brisbane clan's castle. I hazarded a glance up, watching as the wall crumbled—and the shifters on top plummeted into the rubble below.

What a fucking thing to wake up to.

The impact's aftershocks rumbled through our camp, vibrating up into the mountains around us, in violent tremors that sent the guards scrambling for footing. When things somewhat settled down, I spied my dragon racing for the battered wall, a handful of supernaturals behind him, and they hastily dragged enormous chunks of wood, stone, and iron off the wounded dragon shifters that were trapped beneath it all.

"Is it Abramelin?" one of the witches in my protective bubble asked.

"Has he found us?"

"What the hell was that?"

"I know pretty much the same as you guys," I said amidst the rapid-fire interrogation. "My best guess is yes, Abramelin has found us. His roving band of assholes are probably here to take out the Brisbane clan."

Though I had no idea if the Archmage knew that the dragons would have some serious back-up in the form of our militia and various other shifter clans. Hopefully, that was an unpleasant surprise.

"Prepare for battle," I hissed. I then dropped the ward and shot off toward Darius. Above, a shadow moved across the camp, like storm clouds rolling in to blot out the sun, only it wasn't storm clouds. A quick glance up and my heart skipped a beat. "Gargoyles! Turn your spells *upward*!"

A shit ton of gargoyles. Like biblical locusts swarming an Egyptian village.

"Fuck me," I whispered, hurling a disorientating hex into the sky. The gargoyle it hit plummeted to the ground, where militia members tore it apart. The scouts higher up had finally bounced back from the earth-shaking aftershocks and were giving the creatures hell with their guns—automatics, rifles, handguns. They were surprisingly effective.

Although I was still mildly off-balance, considering I'd just woken up, I was pleased to see the militia sprang into action right away. The air was full of magic, colors shooting through the air and picking off gargoyles with more precision than I could have imagined.

With Darius in sight and appearing uninjured, I whirled around and scanned the area for the other most important person in my life.

"Catriona?!"

"I'm fine!" she shouted from the far side of camp. I found her after a few seconds of looking, her hands bright with magic and Quinn by her side. He yanked off his shirt and jeans, and within seconds his human form swelled into a massive navy-blue dragon. His color contrasted sharply with Darius's, but it was still beautiful. The colors rippled with each slight movement, reminding me of gasoline spilled across pavement on a stormy day—a rainbow of color, pinks and purples and dark greens. Blink, and it would be missed.

Dragons really were the most spectacular creatures. Not just for their colors—but for their enormous wingspans and fire-breathing, which Quinn put to use immediately. He shot off, the jump making the ground shake again, and the gusts of air drawn up from his wings nearly sent the gunmen toppling off their perches. I wasn't sure why none of them had shifted yet, but within moments of Quinn's flight, about ten more dragons flew out of the castle, over what was left of their exterior wall, and joined the fight. Gargoyles scattered, letting in the sunrise, but the soft blue dawn of a new day was soon overtaken with flame.

"Are you okay?" Darius called out to me, and I hurried to his side, checking him over for injuries. Although he was a bit dirty, and some of the bits of rock and wood must have nicked his face judging by the small scrapes, he seemed relatively unharmed.

"Are you?" I still asked anyway, letting him assess me just as I'd done to him. "I'm okay. What the fuck?"

"Abramelin," was all he needed to say, and I nodded, my mind chugging along at a thousand miles a second as I considered all the things I needed to do in that moment as the leader of the militia. However, behind me, Quell and Galen seemed to have a handle on things just fine, and for once, I was glad to see them taking charge.

"How did he find us?"

"Doesn't matter now," Darius said gruffly, walking us away from the carnage of what was left of the exterior wall. Behind him, supernaturals continued to pull the wounded out, and I briskly ordered a few fae I knew were adept at healing, Catriona included, to tend to the injured. They snapped to work in a second, Catriona blitzing across the camp with her fae speed to join the others.

"We have to stop him."

"He'll want to breach the castle," Darius told me. "It goes deep into the mountain... There are hundreds of clan members down there, Kaye. We can't let them get past the camp."

"Then those dragons better keep the gargoyles at bay," I said, swallowing my panic at the thought of how many innocent, non-warrior beings resided inside that structure. No wonder they had such hardcore security everywhere. "Do the other clans know?"

"Yeah, I think so."

"Then let's get to it," I managed, sounding more confident than I felt. "Just like before. Me and you. We got this, Darius."

"Kaye." He grabbed me before I could take off running across our destroyed camp, ready to join the others. Across the way, there was a gap between the two mountains. Catriona and I had explored it last night: it opened to another huge gorge within the mountain range. Unlike the previous valley with the Archeri, this was just rock and rubble and loose gravel, with a sea of scraggly yellowish-green, thorny plants everywhere. Not exactly an ideal battleground, but what place ever was?

"What?" I was already panting, the adrenaline fueling my body, that silly inner voice calling for the blood of any who would harm a dragon—*my* dragon, in particular.

"We do this together," he murmured, his hand tightening around my wrist. I glanced down to where we were joined, then nodded.

"Together." I wanted to kiss him, to hug him—just in case I never had the chance again. The sheer number of gargoyles above, paired with the sounds of imminent battle through the narrow passageway between the mountains in the valley beyond —it sounded like the first attack on the hive. This wasn't some petty hit.

This was the real deal.

And there was no time for one last kiss.

There was no time to even consider it.

We tore off after half the militia, led by Quell, who were ready to join the fight outside. Behind us, Galen kept those more magically inclined back, projecting wards over the castle, but even as the first went up, out of the corner of my eye, I spied a witch on a broomstick pummeling it with an array of powerful spell-work. Each time a blast of light hit, it was like a bomb connecting with its target. I couldn't even fathom using my heightened senses here. I'd go insane.

"Kaye!" I tried to peer over the militia at the sound of Quell calling my name. He shot up, wings out and flapping so fast they were just two blurs on either side of him. He cupped his hands around his mouth. "Your brother!"

"Zayne..." I pushed through anyone in my way. I'd been so preoccupied with the *now,* that I hadn't even had time to worry about where my brother was and why he hadn't arrived at the Brisbane clan's castle around the same time we did. As I squeezed through the passageway, wide enough to fit about six people across, but currently inundated with supernaturals trying to get into the fray in the valley, a moment of crippling panic gripped me. *What if Quell was trying to tell me Zayne was hurt? What if he was dead?*

The panic dispersed as quickly as it appeared when Zayne stumbled into the entrance of the narrow passage.

"Zayne!"

I fell into his arms for a moment, hugging him tighter than I'd ever held him before, fighting back tears. Over his shoulder, all hell had broken loose: the chaos I'd woken up to was nothing by comparison. There had to be hundreds of Abramelin's forces storming the valley—but there were hundreds of shifters, along with our supernatural militia, there to push them back.

Magic thickened the air, painting it with broad strokes of color as both sides flung spells back and forth, ground forces coming to blows with weaponry of all kinds. Fleeting beams of sunlight glinted off swords. Gunfire rang out in an already piercingly loud atmosphere. Arrows sliced through flashes of magic.

"Oh, my god," I breathed. "This is madness."

"This is war," Zayne whispered back, "but I am glad to see you're okay."

For now. I almost said it, but I knew it wouldn't do either of us any good. Instead, I pulled free from his embrace and looked him over. While his face had a bit of grizzled scruff to it, he appeared unscathed, though definitely tired. Given that the Sanctius clan held us up for obvious reasons, I suspected Zayne and his group made it to a greater number of shifter clans than we did.

"When did you get here?"

"About ten minutes ago," he told me. "We received your

message yesterday and had to make some last-minute adjustments, but we brought many different shifter clans with us. Paired with yours and the ones who were already here, I think we stand more than a fighting chance."

"And Abramelin?" I scanned the skies as supernaturals from my militia darted around us, racing down the gentle slope toward the unfolding battle in the valley below. I didn't know what I expected, but I pictured the Archmage hovering there on top of a black cloud, watching everything unfold.

"He isn't here, as far as I know."

I nodded. "Well, then that improves our odds."

"Only slightly."

A bellow sounded from above, like the cracking of thunder, and we all looked up to see a little purple dragon swarmed by so many gargoyles, that she lost altitude and plummeted into the valley. The ground trembled beneath us when she collided with the mountainside, but what hurt the most was seeing at least three dozen gargoyles following behind, trying to rip her to pieces.

But not for long.

Darius raced by us with a snarl that sent a chill through my body, shifting mid-run from human to dragon. His flame surged down the hillside, engulfing the gargoyles in flame as the wounded dragon cried out. I felt that cry in my soul, and I found my legs moving of their own accord, like there was an invisible tether connecting the fallen dragon to me—and I had to help her.

"Kaye." Zayne's hand on my shoulder, hard and firm, stopped me. "He's got it covered."

Darius slammed into the cluster of animated stone gargoyles, knocking them off the smaller purple dragon with his head, his spiked tail, and his enormous feet. His war cry sounded across the entire valley.

"What's the plan here, Sis?"

"Protect the castle," I said absently, watching as the smaller dragon shifted back to her human form, and curled into a ball amid all the chaos around her. A few hard blinks and I looked back to Zayne. "There are a lot of non-warriors in there. Darius's father thinks it's key we protect the largest shifter clan, because that'll be Abramelin's primary target."

"Agreed."

More dragons poured out of the mountain range, as if answering Darius's summons—dragons who weren't all part of the Sanctius clan, at that.

"Those are Brisbane fighters," I said quickly, motioning for a few lingering fairies to join me. "Protect the castle, Zayne."

"And eliminate the ground forces," he fired back. "We need the numbers on our side!"

"Got it!"

I zipped down the path, my gait unsteady, with tiny rocks and bits of gravel underfoot.

"Get away from her!" I shouted, hurling a pulse of white magic at the gargoyles closing in on the wounded shifter. My fae back-up did the same, and the sheer force behind the magic sent all the gargoyles, even those grappling with a *very* pissed off Darius, tumbling down the hill, eventually turning to dust.

The injured shifter stayed curled into a tight ball, blood oozing out of the wounds on her back, her hips, and her shoulders.

"Heal her," I ordered, "and then take her back to the castle."

"I can fight," she insisted weakly. Slowly, she lifted her head, gazing up at me with caramel brown eyes swimming with tears. "I can do this."

I hesitated, looking to Darius for confirmation, but he was already fixed on the next battle: the colossal skirmish raging within the valley. We had to be there—we both had to move on. So, I looked to Erik, who had recently healed himself from his spider bite, and nodded.

"Once she's good to go, rejoin the fight and don't leave her side."

He crouched at the shifter's side, slowly running his hands along her trembling body, palms glowing with white magic. "Got it, Kaye."

Leaving the fallen dragon in Erik's very capable hands, I ran after Darius, who was already thundering down into the valley. His war cry rallied a few dragons hanging back picking off gargoyles; they answered the call with bellows of their own. A veritable symphony of mighty dragons, their hearts on display for all to hear.

The ground forces locked in battle with Abramelin's cretins —a mix of demons, witches, ghouls, goblins, gremlins... the works. The area was basically a giant melting pot of bodies and magic and blades. To call it overwhelming to the senses was the biggest fucking understatement of the year. I slowed to a jog, trying to assess where I was most needed, and quickly realized there were dozens of smaller battles that could use my help. Shifter scents, supernatural ethnicities—I felt them all, wave after wave of identifications, tugging me this way and that. Some of the shifters fought hand-to-hand in their human forms, while some shifters appeared in their animal forms; nearby, a pack of white wolves ran down a demon fleeing on all fours, his body contorted and twisted into a backward crab-walk as he tried to outrun them.

Tried and failed. Within seconds the pack closed in, hunting in perfect synchronicity, tearing the demon's rotting gray flesh from his bones.

"Go up," I shouted to Darius. He too, hadn't directly entered the skirmish, but instead appeared to be evaluating everything— and fending off a horde of goblins with lazy flicks of his tail. Each hit knocked them down, and a few seconds later they scrambled to their feet, knives in hand, and tried to attack again —only to be knocked down again. I blasted the group with a stunning spell, and unlike the brute impact of Darius's spiked tail, this time they stayed down. He glanced back, as if I'd shooed away the flies, and huffed out a cloud of black smoke.

I knew that look. Darius wasn't happy with the idea of being separated.

"We'll still fight together," I argued, pointing skyward. "There are a lot of witches up there we need to eliminate. I'll stay within your shadow." I dodged a rogue arrow, feeling a soft *whoosh* as it whizzed by my head.

"Sorry!" a distracted elf called from the edge of the battle. "*Someone* threw me off balance."

A demon cackled, only to be impaled mid-laugh by a dwarf's axe.

How the hell was any of this normal? At this point, it didn't faze me.

And I couldn't decide whether that was okay or not.

"Go," I shouted, feeling the magic crackle within my palms, like the kindling of a freshly lit fire. Darius's wings snapped out, and I set a hand against one. "Just look for your shadow. I'll be there."

He must have taken me at my word, because moments later he was airborne and barbecuing a hovering quartet of witches.

"Okay," I whispered to myself. "Now... Kaye, where do *you* fit in here?"

I hadn't taken more than two steps toward a fox shifter and a herd of goblins engaged in hand-to-hand combat, when a blast of magic slammed into my shoulder. A hard breath shot out of me when I hit the ground, little jagged rocks biting into my hands as I steadied myself.

"You just don't go down easily, do you?" someone sneered. I whipped back, recognizing the voice immediately, but not believing it for a second—not until I laid eyes on the one fae I could have sworn, would be cowering far, far away from war.

"Jasmine?" I shot to my feet, fueling myself with defensive white magic in case she tried to sucker-spell me again. "W-What are you doing here?"

"You know, I thought my gargoyle was better at hunting filthy half-breeds," she spat, picking at her perfectly manicured nails. She wore her jet-black hair in a braided crown around her head, and while I was still in my sleeping attire—a long black shirt and a pair of faded jeans—she was dressed like the warlocks I'd seen during the first attack on the hive. Leather armor. Dark colors. Pants instead of her usual mini-dresses. A billowing dark gray cape fluttered behind her—too dramatic for some, but just right for a fae like Jasmine. Her delicate features seemed almost hawkish and sharp with the war paint across her cheeks, as if she'd used the ink to contour her face to its best angles.

"*You* sent the gargoyle?" I demanded, my brain snapping back to reality and accepting that this wasn't just a bad dream, as I recalled how this all had started for me when the mysterious package had arrived outside my apartment door. It felt like so long ago, yet it had only been a couple of months. "*Why?*"

"Because my uncle gave me a whole army of them to use as I wished," she told me, her tone casual, like we were chatting about shoes or television shows. "And I *wished* to eliminate the half-breed shifter who was sleeping with my disgusting ex-boyfriend."

The purse of her lips gave her away, and I managed to whip up a shield of white magic when she hurled a hex at me. Bright green magic pounded into my shield, fizzling out like a dying firework. Powerful. I hadn't expected that.

"Your uncle?" I swallowed hard, struggling to reconcile these two realities. In the one I'd always thought to be true, Jasmine was nothing more than a stuck-up, rude little bitch. She dressed well, primped regularly, and was a total buzzkill at parties when she made every conversation about her. *This* Jasmine was hard to accept, the one standing before me in war paint proclaiming her uncle was—

"Abramelin," Jasmine remarked with a giggle. "He lets me do whatever I want, and right now, I want to do what my gargoyle didn't. Say goodbye to your dragon, half-breed."

She hurled another hex, one right after the other, and stalked toward me. The closeness intensified the magic, and I struggled to hold her back, to keep her vile curses from striking me. In the sunlight, I could see my white magic peel and bubble, like it was freshly applied window tint on a car's windshield and some asshole decided they wanted to pick at it before it dried.

"Jasmine," I choked out, my arms wavering under the tremendous pressure of maintaining my shield, "I know we haven't seen eye-to-eye in the past—" She scoffed and rolled her eyes, to which I had to agree. "Okay, well. *Ever.* But can't you see that this is *insanity*? I don't want to fight you—"

"Oh, blah, blah, blah," she half-shouted, scratching at my wall of white magic with her perfectly manicured nails before hitting me with a double-whammy curse and hex, a blend of purple and green light twining together and slamming into my shield. "So boring. Save your sanctimonious bullshit for your band of feeble-minded followers."

"You're one to talk about feeble-minded followers," I grumbled. Knowing I couldn't hold my protective barrier much longer, I decided to let go—and act.

My inner voice applauded.

Taking the opportunity to strike between her spellcasting, I dropped my shield and pummeled her with a disorienting hex, paired with a pulse of magic. The combination sent her flying—like a big magical fist that knocked her on her ass *and* made her head spin.

"I don't want to fight you," I insisted. While I knew that *she* knew I'd always disliked her, I hoped Jasmine could see the olive branch I was trying to extend. "Jasmine, please, we can talk like civilized—"

"Don't you *dare* mention the word *civilized* in my presence," the fae spat as she clambered to her feet, aggressively swiping aside hair loosened from her crown. "Your mother bred with some disgusting *animal* and didn't have the decency to end you before your miserable life began. *You* are far from civilized."

Well then. That's how it was going to be, huh?

I blocked a hex, the ball of deathly orange light bouncing off my white-magic-surrounded fist and disappearing. It was clear where Jasmine stood; no amount of reasoning was going to change that. So, I resigned myself to just survive. If she ended up dead in the process, I'd try to keep my widow's wail to a minimum.

Unfortunately, it quickly became clear that Jasmine was better at magic than I was—and really, how could she not be, given that her uncle was the fucking Archmage responsible for this mess. With every spell, or curse, or hex that I managed to block, usually in the nick of time, she had another one raring to go. Most of my offensive magic was deflected with more skill, more strength. It seemed my moment of victory with the curse combo was doomed to be short-lived.

I cried out when a blast of red light hit me, catching me just as I tried to throw up another shield. It sent me flying backward and landing hard on my side, hip and shoulder screaming in pain. I winced at the feel of hundreds of tiny cuts, like an army of paper cuts, appeared across every bit of exposed skin.

A cruel curse, but from Jasmine, I expected no less. She giggled, her hands raised as if to finish me, and I threw up a weak shield, hoping that would do—then stared in amazement as about ten ravens dive-bombed her in unison.

Shifters. I could sense them. They ripped at her hair, her skin, her clothes. A few brave ones went for her eyes. I used the distraction to bolster my defenses, and when she finally managed to cast them away, her eyes held that special storm of crazy that should have sent me running.

Only they didn't—and Jasmine quickly realized why.

I had something Jasmine would never have.

Friends who would always have my back.

I sensed them coming before I saw them: a whole cluster of my militia, storming up from the valley, metaphorically rolling up their sleeves, ready to get their hands dirty. Overhead, Darius's roar rang out, and I squinted up as his shadow passed by.

Bleeding and exhausted, I let my shield drop when he landed, the ground thundering beneath him.

"Easy there, Kaye," Erik ordered, jogging to my side and quickly healing my injuries. Behind him, the female dragon I'd rescued earlier scowled at Jasmine, her eyes darkened and black smoke coiled from her nostrils. I sensed she was about two seconds away from shifting, and bit back a smile when that beautiful purple dragon emerged, her cry forcing Jasmine to clamp her hands down over her ears. Erik helped me to my feet, and after thanking him, I hurried over to Darius. The moment I touched his wing, he shifted back.

"You okay?" he muttered as I hurried to his side. I nodded, letting him kiss my cheek quickly, feeling the flow of magic simmering behind me as my back-up readied the best weapon at their disposal.

"*Ugh,*" Jasmine groaned. She then looked very pointedly at Darius's nude figure. "You shifters are such vile creatures."

"Jasmine," Darius said curtly, face pinched in anger. "*Stop* this! So many innocents are being destroyed, and for what?"

"Innocents? Are you for real?" she snarled, hands pulsing with a bright orange magic whose vibrations made my stomach turn. "Do you not recall what your filthy kind did to my family?"

"Jasmine..." For a fleeting moment, I felt sorry for her. It was the slight quiver in her voice that got me. "The actions of the few don't reflect the thoughts of the many. I'm sorry—"

All my compassion flew out the window when she hurled two blasts of orange magic our way, the curses searing the white magic shield I barely threw up in time. My gaze narrowed as I watched her twist in rage, her chest heaving. The whites of her eyes appeared somewhat reddened—as though on the verge of tears. I couldn't blame her, not entirely. I'd always envisioned Jasmine as a heartless fae and nothing more. It was hard to imagine her having genuine feelings, real emotions, for someone other than herself.

"I don't need your *pity*, you animal," Jasmine sneered. "I don't need it from either of you. All I need is for you, all of you, to pay your blood debts for the lives you took!"

She fired off another hex; this time one aimed squarely at Darius. I pushed him out of the way, managing to deflect it just in time, hackles up at the thought of her targeting him with magic. The beam of coppery light bounced straight back at her, but she absorbed her revolting magic with a shudder.

"So, you'd sacrifice the lives of thousands to make up for the actions of a few?" Darius snapped, shouldering his way to my side again, his expression a blend of fury and disbelief. "Jasmine, I know you don't agree with what your uncle is doing. You know this is wrong."

"The lives of six supernatural beings are equivalent to the thousands of shifters we plan to eliminate," she said icily. My jaw dropped, but before she could hurl another hex our way, my militia back-up had apparently had enough: they pummeled her with magic, relentlessly. The first few spells she deflected, but eventually, they pushed her back—and I saw the panic in her eyes.

She thought they were going to kill her.

And I saw no reason to stop them.

Shrieking in fear, perhaps some fury too, Jasmine threw her gray cape around her body. The fabric swirled like a mini-tornado, growing tighter and tighter around her—until Jasmine and her cape disappeared into thin air.

I shook my head in disbelief. "I... I have no words."

"Where the hell did she go?" Darius asked. "Can you do that? Disappear into thin air?"

"She teleported to God-knows-where. And no, I haven't learned that yet."

"Good. I have a hard enough time keeping track of you as it is," Darius grumbled under his breath, and I chuckled. We exchanged short-lived, weary grins before I urged the others to rejoin the battle, and thanked them for having my back.

"Anytime, Kaye," Hazel, a witch with the bluest eyes I'd ever seen, remarked. She then hurled an impressive lightning-bolt shaped hex into the air and knocked down two witches circling us. They slammed into the gravelly terrain like dead weight.

Right. Back to business then.

"How's everything going up there?" I asked, knowing Darius would have to return to the skies immediately. He shook his head, his eyes dark.

"I don't know where Abramelin found all these gargoyles, but they just keep coming."

"He probably created them himself," I noted. "Or, at the very least, his warlocks did. These all can't be stolen from church rooftops and such."

He shrugged. "You never know."

"They're not."

"Maybe—"

I screamed when a shockwave blasted across the valley, the sheer magnitude of the explosion sending Darius and I flying in opposite directions. It radiated across the battlefield, knocking down all those in its path.

"Jesus *fuck*," Darius growled noisily, flopping onto his back and groaning. Fearing the worst, I scrambled to my feet and raced toward him—only to find him clutching his manhood and cringing in pain. *Right*. This wasn't exactly a forgiving landscape for exposed genitals to slam into.

"Can I, er..." I hesitated, not exactly sure what to do for him, but he waved me off gruffly, cheeks red.

"It's fine," he managed. "What the hell was that?"

"It came from the castle," I told him, offering a hand and helping him up. When he was steady, I dusted myself off and turned toward the Brisbane stronghold. "I've never felt anything so powerful before."

Sparks and twisted coils of magic shot out from the destroyed passageway that had led to our campsite; in its place was a gaping hole, bits of mountain scattered around the magical bomb that had created such carnage. Two figures battled in what was once the very throughway Zayne and I had reunited. The crackle and sizzle of competing magic like the boom of thunder, even all the way down the hill. I enhanced my senses, honing in on the figures with my second sight, then cried out when I realized who it was: my careless, half-brother fighting an Archmage.

The Archmage, I assumed.

"I think that's Abramelin," I gasped. "He's... He's going to kill Zayne!"

It wasn't that I had no faith in my brother's abilities, but this was *Abramelin*. Swathed in black fabric, the Archmage had Jasmine's slanted, slim facial features and birdlike eyes—narrowed and unblinking, seeped with intelligence and fire. He wore his hair in a crew-cut fashion, and his cheeks were clean-shaven, save for a patch of black hair on his chin. In a conventional sense, I might have called him handsome. But none of that mattered. He was a raging psychopath, who wielded magic like a second skin.

Darius grabbed me before I could take off, and I glared, trying to wrench my arm free. "Let go!"

"We do this together, Kaye," he insisted once again, his voice tinged with that fierce baritone rumble that set my heart aflame. "We do it together, or not at all."

"I know, Darius. Together. Let's go!"

He released me for a moment, and I ducked out of the way as he shifted forms. Within seconds, his sunset coloring rippled beside me and I clambered up his side, carefully avoiding the spikes along his spine, and situated myself at the nape of his neck.

"Go!" I cried, then clung to him as he shot off the ground. I tightened my thighs and held on for dear life. Riding a dragon was like riding the world's most insane motorcycle, without a helmet. I narrowed my eyes, bracing against the wind. While fae speed might have gotten me there just as fast, I wouldn't trade Darius's ability to breathe Archmage-melting fire for anything. He exhaled vibrant blue flame down on Abramelin as I screamed for Zayne to get out of the way. My brother, bloodied but still swinging, leaped back as the fire surged toward the Archmage. However, before impact, Abramelin threw up a shield, and the fire peeled around him like rain spilling down a sturdy umbrella.

From above, I took in Zayne's militia and Abramelin's men battling in the courtyard of the castle, their fight spilling into our old campsite. Each beat of Darius's enormous wings sent rubble and debris flying. When his fire-breath fizzled, Abramelin was ready. He hurled up a blast of bright blue light from both hands, and I felt the heat of his magic, the raw power of it, before it was anywhere near us.

Darius swerved hard to avoid it, but the hex carved across the side of his belly, leaving a bloody slice in its wake. My dragon lost his balance, bellowing in pain, and I lost my hold in the process, falling from his neck and slamming into the ground. I exhaled sharply, as if to breathe out the pain, then staggered to my feet.

"Back off, Kaye!" Zayne shouted. The two were back at it again now that Abramelin had dealt with me and Darius—like we were nothing. "You're no match for him!"

"That's right," Abramelin purred, his voice carrying over the sizzle and snap of spells colliding. "Your mongrel sister has no place here among *true* magic-wielders."

I was *not* a mongrel. My eyes narrowed as an untapped rage coursed through me. I'd had enough of this. Enough of people like Jasmine and Abramelin.

And my inner voice agreed.

Take him down. For good.

"Fuck you, Abramelin." I hurled one disorienting hex right after the other, rapid-fire, as Zayne pitched in with a few spells of his own. The Archmage weaved and dodged, but only barely managed to escape the assault unsinged. Overhead, Darius had regained his balance, though that didn't stop the large red droplets of blood from watering the ground, the open wound on his side desperate for my attention. But I couldn't give it. I couldn't tear myself away from the fight with Abramelin—not for one second.

My dragon seemed to know that. Zayne must have too, because he stopped shouting for me to leave and welcomed my help.

And so, began a grand dance between us four, Abramelin in the belly of our Bermuda's triangle. Zayne and I worked in tandem, hurling whatever we had at him, and Darius kept Abramelin's minions from joining the fight. Although the three of us said nothing to one another—nor did we respond to Abramelin's maniacal villain goading, no matter how much his words stung—we succeeded in steering him slowly, but surely, away from the Brisbane castle.

But the Archmage was exceptionally skilled. He fended off two streams of constant magical attacks, plus a dragon, like it was all child's play. As far as I could tell, he hadn't even broken a sweat, while dodging hexes and hurling them straight back at all three of us.

I, on the other hand, was drenched in the early morning sunshine, the sweat soaking through my clothes. No matter, we fought on, whether a victory was possible or not. The rest of the world fell away as we battled, as we avoided harrowing curses that charred our clothes and scalded our skin, as Darius did his best to fight the realm's best Archmage with no more than brute strength and skill.

Our luck was bound to run out, of course, and when it did, I went down hard. A non-fatal, though still painful, hex nailed me right in the chest. I gasped, trying to swallow down air, and watched as Zayne went down next, followed by Darius, whose collision with the ground rocked the valley. I tried to push myself up, but Abramelin leapt—literally, like a grasshopper—from his spot some twenty feet away and landed on top of me, pinning me to the gravelly earth below.

"You'll have to go first, half-breed," he hissed, pressing a hard hand to my throat, the other raised, a ball of black energy forming in his palm. His eye twitched as he studied me, face rampant with disgust. "You see, I'd like your brother to watch you die, along with your filthy lover." He moved in closer, hovering above my face, his rank breath filling my nostrils as I struggled for air. "You're nothing to me, of course. Just a gnat. One beast of many, I'll slaughter before the day is out. But to them, you're everything. To them, you're the world."

Abramelin howled right in my face, spittle coating my skin, and I struggled to free myself.

"But you aren't the world," he hissed, his lip twitching. "You're nothing more than an abomination, and I will see that your kind never tarnishes our realm again..."

It was then that I caught it—the glint of sunlight reflecting off the massive knife on his belt. As he crushed my windpipe in his strong grip, still ranting on about my filthy mother and the blemish my existence had created on the supernatural world, I jerked the knife free, then unceremoniously plunged it straight up into his gut.

Hot blood spilled down my hand, and I wriggled away when he released me. The shock registered just as plainly as his disgust once had, riddled all over his face as the glowing black ball of magic shrunk and disappeared into his palm.

"Y-You..." he stammered, and I kicked away from him when he tried to grab me again, then scrambled back as quickly as I could.

"Me," I growled, then watched as he slowly withdrew the knife, blood puddling beneath him. I smirked when his narrowed gaze shot up to mine. "I'm the last thing you'll ever see. *Me*. The half-breed that destroyed you."

The black magic surged again, this time in both hands as the knife clattered to the ground. Seconds later, however, a blast of bright blue flame engulfed him, and I lifted a hand to shield my eyes. When it extinguished, the ash of the great, psychopathic Archmage, Abramelin billowed across the valley—already forgotten.

Knowing I hadn't a moment to lose, I was on my feet in a flash and tending to Darius's wounds. Once I sealed the gaping cut on his side, I checked on Zayne. While he'd seen better days, my brother was alive, mentally sound, and relatively unscathed from our skirmish with Abramelin. It was more than any of us could have asked for.

"What now?" I asked, still trying to catch my breath from the whole ordeal, hands planted on my hips. We looked to the fighting in the valley, which hadn't slowed one bit, then to the half-demolished Brisbane castle at the top of the hill where Abramelin's warlock cronies had gathered, perhaps hoping he'd annihilate my brother.

"We continue keeping people safe," Zayne remarked. His exhaustion was plain as day. "His people are going to keep fighting until we stop them."

Darius roared—an excessive reaction to our muted conversation, and a quick glance up the hill told me why. All of Abramelin's warlocks and various other supernatural cronies charged toward us like the goddamn cavalry. Maybe they had seen their master fall, but regardless, his message of hate lived on.

"Out of the fucking frying pan and into the fire," I grumbled, brushing the hair away from my sweaty forehead. I was running on empty, my stomach in desperate need of food and water, but if I wanted to *live* to satiate it, I couldn't stop fighting. Not yet, anyway, no matter how desperately, I wanted to collapse and go back to sleep.

A strangled cackle slipped out, and I clamped a hand over my mouth when Zayne shot me a curious look.

But the thought of just going to sleep, like I wouldn't be wracked with nightmares for weeks, was totally cackle-worthy.

Summoning a curse that would temporarily blind our assailants, I hurled the bright orb of cerulean toward Abramelin's captains. One raised his hand to block it, but the curse exploded into a fine dust over its targets, catching them all in its web. I straightened my sore shoulders, grinning.

Behind the dark-robed warlocks, dragons poured from the mountains, sandwiching them in between us. Darius took to the skies, his blue flame cutting the group in half, and I gasped when he narrowly avoided a black flash of hateful magic—the kind that might have stopped his heart had it been a direct hit. Fearing for him, for all us of against Abramelin's elite, I got to work on protection wards, while Zayne met the warlocks in a full-on magical assault.

As I drew from my limited white magic within, a haze materialized in front of me. At first, I thought it was a trick of the sun, or maybe my wearied brain had just had enough, but slowly the dark purple fog thickened—and sprouted into a man.

A djinn, to be specific.

He cocked his head to the side, a twisted grin on his lips, that little ponytail flicking rather dramatically, and then latched onto my wrist before I could react. My scream died in my throat, and I watched, horrified, as blackness crept through the veins along my arm, a terrifying coldness accompanying it. A djinn's touch was poison, more than the bite of an Arachne, and as I fell hard into darkness, the last thing on my mind was that a djinn's touch —was fatal.

❦ 12 ❦

I AWOKE IN A DIMLY LIT, worryingly-quiet, room—feeling like I'd been hit by a freight train.

Was this the afterlife?

No. If I were dead, I wouldn't be in pain.

Unless I was in Hell: a realm for paranoid humans that I'd never believed in, even as a supernatural being.

"Kaye?"

A soft moan crept up my throat in response, though it died on the tip of my tongue. I tried my hardest to get my eyes open, to make them stay open, but the throbbing pain throughout my body was coming into sharper focus and logic told me to succumb to sleep, to ride it out.

But I couldn't.

That was Darius's worried voice—and Darius couldn't be in Hell. My hands scrambled along the scratchy quilt thrown over me, my fingers frantic to find him in the darkness.

"Hey, hey, it's okay. Calm down," came his rumbly, baritone admonishment. My heart stopped racing the moment our hands found one another, his engulfing mine in a soothing heat that I wanted to feel all over.

"D-Darius?" A raspy croak—that was the best I could do, but

his soft chuckle made me feel better about it. A shadow loomed overhead when I finally managed to force my eyes open, at least halfway, and I realized it was him reaching over me. Moments later, the dim lighting lifted somewhat, and I noted that he had been fiddling with an oil lamp of some kind on a wooden bedside table. The flame brightened, it's glow dancing over his handsome features.

"Hi," I whispered, smiling even though it made my face hurt. "Am I... Am I alive?"

"For now," he murmured, settling on the edge of the snug twin bed I found myself in. "You scared the absolute shit out of me though."

"It was a djinn." My heartbeat quickened again as the memory, foggy yet present, filtered into my mind's eye. "H-He—"

"He touched you," my dragon finished for me. "I saw it. Zayne got him before the poison could get too far. I tried to get to you, but there were so many of Abramelin's men in the way... I couldn't." His grip tightened. "It was the most fucking terrifying moment of my life, Kaye."

"Tell me about it," I rasped, a breathy chuckle slipping out when I saw him smile. "Seriously. I thought I was dead. I saw the poison... I..." I blinked hard as I remembered all that had happened. "Wait. Did we win? Is Abramelin dead?"

I'd watched him die, but that certainly hadn't stopped the fighting. *Where was Zayne? Was Catriona okay?* Panic jolted through me, more poignant than any of my physical pains. I hadn't seen her since I sent her to tend to those that had fallen at the castle wall—and there had been that explosion, the one before I saw Zayne fighting Abramelin. *What if—*

"Kaye, easy. Breathe." My dragon pulled me away from the brink, silencing my racing thoughts as he stroked my wrists with his thumbs. His voice calmed me, quieted the fear, and I took a few deep breaths alongside him. When we finished, he leaned down to kiss each of my hands, then sat up with a grin.

"Abramelin's dead. His forces turned tail and ran when they realized they were a headless snake. Catriona is safe. Quinn too. Zayne was wounded, but not gravely... All is well in the world. Finally."

I let myself sink back into a plush pillow, considering his words—and remembering his father's sentiment about peace. There was never any peace. Just a fool's peace. Just because Abramelin had fallen, certainly didn't mean there wasn't another crazy warlock or mage itching to take his place.

My eyelids weighed heavy suddenly. The longer I let myself dwell on it, the heavier they became. Clearly, I had been saved from the djinn's poison, but I imagined recovery from that kind of attack wouldn't be easy. My gaze wandered to Darius's face, eager to distract myself with more pleasant things. It was then that a memory struck, foggy just like the last one—fading in and out of view. A man. A dragon carrying me through the battlefield, my arms hanging limp.

"Thank you for saving me," I whispered, voice breaking. Tears blurred my vision, falling when I closed my eyes as Darius kissed me.

"I'd love to take credit for that, Kaye, my fae," he told me, "but I'm afraid it wasn't me."

My eyebrows twitched upward curiously. Sleep clawed at me, pulling me back, and my body was all too willing to fall. It needed the time to heal. I could give it that—in a minute.

"Then w-who?"

"Well, my love, you seem to have a knack for trapping alpha shifters in your gravitational pull," he teased, sitting up and glancing back. I couldn't bring much of the dark room into focus, but I detected a slight movement in the shadows. Another being. A shifter. A dragon. Darius smiled at the newcomer, then turned to me. "Brisbane's very own alpha, practically annihilated anyone within a five-foot radius of you when you passed out. Zayne took care of the djinn, and I had to watch him heroically rush you back to the castle."

There was an edge to his voice; while Darius seemed to be trying to keep the story light and teasing, he didn't feel that way about it. Not completely.

Darius would always come back for me.

I imagined he was pissed someone beat him to it.

I knew I would be, had our positions been reversed.

"Now, Kaye, he's here to meet you," Darius told me, his voice gentler now—like he was walking on eggshells, "and, well, he's..."

My eyes darted to the man at the end of my bed as the rest of the world seemed to fade away. The darkness had won once more. My body would get its peace. Yet as my vision clouded and the tension eased out of my limbs, succumbing to the sweet embrace of a healing sleep, that *face* remained so startling clear. Like I had been searching for it my whole life. My inner voice said nothing, yet I felt her calm, her clarity—her connection to this stranger who stood at the foot of the bed.

"I-I know him," I whispered, my words like thunder in my ears—yet in reality like the softest drizzle of spring mist. "He's my father..."

And with that, I was gone, this time knowing that I wouldn't awaken to the midnight of my own death.

I'd wake to the dawn of my new life.

❦   13   ❦

"ARE you sure you don't want me to stay?"

I grinned, hugging Zayne tighter, despite the dull ache blistering throughout my body.

"Of course, I *want* you to stay, you idiot," I whispered, "but I don't *need* you to stay. Alfheim needs you more than I do."

"You sure?" Behind him, I spied Darius embracing his friend, Colton, briefly before moving on to Liam. One of them said something and all three burst out into laughter—a sight that made my heart sing. Seeing genuine joy on Darius's face after all the bullshit we'd been through… Well, it somehow managed to make everything better.

"Positive," I murmured. We held one another a few moments longer, then eased apart, with Zayne gently holding me by my upper arms as I found my balance again.

After a week of healing in a dimly lit room, with only the Brisbane healers, Darius, Zayne, and Catriona for company, today was my first day outside again. Having lived in darkness, fighting for my life as healers extracted the poison from my system, the outside world was kind of overwhelming. A startlingly bright sun beat down on the mountainside, a landscape that was green and vibrant and thriving. Situated on the other side of the Brisbane clan's castle, it was where the other shifter clans had camped out before the grand battle, right at the front door. It was gorgeous out here—beautiful, yet draining. Even though I had fought to be here, to say farewell to my brother, the militia, and all the shifters who had risked their lives for our cause, I quickly found myself wanting to sit in the shade and watch from a distance instead.

"If he were anyone else, I wouldn't leave you here," Zayne told me softly, nodding in Darius's direction. "But I know, he'll take good care of you."

"And I'll take care of him," I countered with a cheeky grin. My brother's hand fell to my elbow as I swayed, and he gave it a quick squeeze when I steadied out.

"Let me know if things go south," he insisted. I noticed the somewhat worried look he shot to the castle behind me, wherein my father—like I needed any more of life's curveballs—sat on a throne, lording over the mighty Brisbane clan. "James seems like a good man, a competent alpha, but you never know what happens behind closed doors. Keep your wits about you."

"Of course."

I couldn't help but wonder, if my brother's concerns stemmed from the fact that this man had an affair with our mother, rather than an outright concern for my safety. I had only seen my father—James Holloway, alpha dragon of the Brisbane clan, and my rescuer—the first day I awoke after the battle, but Catriona told me he struck her as kind and thoughtful, a true king among shifters. He and the ruling family had been working hard to tend to those wounded in battle, to feed all the armies, and to send everyone off in better condition than they arrived in.

As I looked around the mountainside, watching as shifter clans hiked off in different directions and supernaturals engaged in whatever magical transport they saw fit, I had to admit that the man ran a tight ship. Everyone looked great, even my brother, who had visited me on my second day of recovery with an enormous wound jetting across his entire face about an inch thick. Today, I could hardly see it.

"Stay in touch," Zayne insisted, kissing both of my cheeks, then my forehead. "We'll see each other soon."

"Very soon," I agreed. "Don't be a stranger again, or I'll be forced to kick your ass. Remember, you taught me how."

We hugged one last time before he jogged off to join Quell, Galen, and all his other captains. Having already said my good-byes to the fae duo, I waved them off, standing on shaky legs, alone, in front of the castle.

As the large groups moved on, one lone figure walked towards me. I held a hand out to Darius as he approached, and he quickened his pace, taking it in both of his and bringing it to his lips to kiss.

"How are you feeling?"

"Tired," I admitted. "When did the sun get so bright?"

"Do you want to meet with James tomorrow instead?" He studied me with concern, eyes sweeping along my arms—looking for the black poison that had once raced through my veins like ice. He'd find nothing today, but I understood his fears. I dreamed about that same blackness every night.

"No," I told him. "I don't want to wait. I need answers. I need... to know..."

Answers such as whether my father had known about my existence and if he had just abandoned me. My family waited beyond the open metal gates; there was no way I was waiting another day to finally meet them.

"I'll be right beside you the entire time," Darius promised, an arm hooked around my waist as we slowly made our way back to the castle. "You say the word, and we bail."

"Pinky promise?" We locked pinkies as a nervous giggle slipped through my lips.

"Forever promise, Kaye."

I squared my shoulders, steeling myself for whatever news

might await me, and picked up my pace, as much as my weakened body would allow.

Time for answers—for better or for worse.

WE HADN'T MADE IT MORE THAN A COUPLE OF STEPS BEYOND the front gates, before Cedric zipped to our sides. The burly dragon was almost taller than Darius, and from what I was told, he was one of the best guards that Brisbane had to offer. He'd been my silent watcher while I healed, standing outside my door and ensuring only approved guests saw me in my weakened state. We hadn't talked much, but the guy, bald as a bowling ball, seemed to take his job very seriously.

And in that moment, his job involved escorting us directly to alpha James Holloway's throne room. He gave a curt nod when Darius issued the order, and we followed him through the unfamiliar castle. While the Sanctius village and their halls had made me think of the Vikings, this one was a straight-up medieval castle – from the little red and white flags fluttering at the top of the towers, to the old cobblestone floors. It descended deep into the mountain, enhanced with magic—I could feel it just about everywhere I went.

As we walked through winding halls and enormous wings on our way to the throne room, we passed Quinn and Catriona. I tried to flag her down, but she was engaged in a game that looked like a blend of hide-and-seek and tag with a bunch of shifter children in a courtyard. Sunlight streamed down onto them. A fountain with a large dragon-shaped spout added soothing background noise to the chorus of childish squeals and giggles. Quinn hovered nearby, watching, not engaging, but I knew a man in love when I saw it. If I hadn't been off to meet my *father*, I might have stopped to watch the love blossom.

Instead, I had to concentrate on the here and now. No matter how the conversation went, I could fill Catriona in on it later—that is, if I even wanted to stay here after all was said and done. This man hadn't been a part of my life *at all* until he rescued me from the djinn. If I learned that he had known about me all along and just didn't care to meet me, I couldn't imagine I'd want much to do with him.

"We can still make a run for it," Darius offered as we approached a set of double doors—dark metal, though thankfully not wrought iron this time. I glanced up at him, wishing he wouldn't make such a tempting offer, and he grinned. "Just kidding. I'll hold tight if you're feeling cagey."

"Thanks." And I meant it. As much as I wanted to confront my father here, I felt as though I'd endured enough conflict, war, and strife in the last few months to last a lifetime. I wasn't sure I could stomach something that threatened to break me again. But, suddenly the doors opened, Cedric the guard gestured for us to enter, and Darius steered me right along. There was no turning back now.

Given the overall look and feel of the Brisbane castle, I'd expected to stumble into a huge, long hall with a throne at the far end. Maybe an enormous fireplace, a couple of dogs napping in the corner, along with banners of all the clan families hanging from the walls. What I found instead was a garden paradise right in the middle of a mountain range. Ivy covered every square inch of wall space, of which there were only three. The fourth side opened into a crystal-clear pool, into which flowed a gentle waterfall from the mountain itself. Fat green lily pads lay scattered on the water's surface, and a lone beam of sunshine filtered in from above.

"Holy... shit." It slipped out before I could stop it. The rest of the hall was one big, wild garden—literally. There were no commercial floral arrangements. No tulips in full bloom. If we weren't in the middle of the mountains, this could very well have been something Mother Nature herself landscaped during some downtime. Long grass reached mid-calf. Pussy willows grew near the pool. Dandelions dotted throughout—weeds to the urban gardener, yet a welcome splash of an uplifting color in this mystic place. Bunches of lavender, that I just wanted to bury my face in, grew everywhere. One would think the smell, the *feel* of so much lush flora, would be overwhelming, but all I felt here was pure, sweet magic.

A magic that made me feel at home. Just like James's face, it was as if this magic had been with me my whole life, always waiting in the wings, there to comfort me in times of stress and cherish me in moments of victory.

"Your mother created the garden on her last visit here," came a deep voice from across the hall. "I've maintained it ever since... in her memory."

I lifted my gaze, searching him out, and when our eyes met, I clutched Darius for support. James stood tall and proud over the sea of greenery. With emerald green eyes like mine, he wore his auburn, red hair back in a ponytail. I'd never looked like Zayne's father, and I'd always wondered why. While my brother and I both had red hair, they weren't the same shade. James's was a near perfect match to mine.

Swallowing hard, I did one last sweep of our surroundings, though this time I didn't take much of it in. Heart pounding, I made my way through the garden, careful not to crush anything underfoot, and stopped a few feet from him. Darius's presence lingered behind me, close enough for support, but far enough back to let me stand on my own two feet.

I loved that about him.

"Hi," I managed, my voice mousier than I would have liked.

"Hi." James's gentle response quieted my racing heart, but only somewhat. I stiffened when he reached out for me, his hand hanging in the tense air between us. Had I honed into my second sight, I imagined I'd see the space pulsating, vibrating, quivering with all the emotions that swirled around this ambiguous relationship with the stranger I suddenly found myself standing before.

Then, with a furrowed brow, he reached out and tenderly

lifted a lock of my hair. Darius cleared his throat behind me, a guttural warning for James to go easy, but the Brisbane alpha paid him no mind. Instead, he rubbed my hair between his fingers, the crinkling sound thunderous in the silence. I stood there, stiff and still, letting him touch me, only releasing the breath I'd been holding when his hand dropped to his side.

I swallowed hard again, unsure what to do, where to start—what to *say*. James breached that barrier first when he grabbed my shoulder, seemingly out of nowhere, and pulled me into his arms. Staring wide-eyed over his shoulder, I didn't react at first, arms limp at my side, back arched as he pulled me against him. Slowly, however, my eyes began to water, and I buried my face against the nape of his neck, against warm skin that smelled like a childhood I'd never truly known, and wrapped my arms around his firm, thick torso.

"Shhh, I know. I know," he murmured, and I felt his hand on the back of my head, holding me as I shook with emotion I hadn't even realized was there. I'd gone my whole life thinking my father, Zayne's father, had abandoned me because I was the reason my mother was dead. That pill had been hard enough to swallow as it was, but I'd done it. I'd tucked it away, never allowing it to hurt me again. And now here, even though James hadn't said more than a few words to me, his presence ripped open all those old wounds, and suddenly I was that confused, shattered little girl again, wishing her daddy would just love her.

On the verge of a breakdown, I eased out of his arms, turned and hastily wiped away the tears streaming down my face. Darius moved toward me, his expression hard, worried, but a slight shake of my head stopped him.

"I didn't mean to... make you cry," James said softly, and I faced him again with a weak laugh.

"I didn't expect to, honestly." Sniffling, I finished cleaning myself up, then extended my hand for him to shake. "Hi. My name's Kaye. I'm... your daughter."

He accepted the gesture with an easy sort of smile, the kind that had never come naturally to Zayne's father when we were alone, and squeezed firmly as we shook hands. "Hello. My name's James, and I'm your father."

"Should we sit?" I looked around for a bench, a high-backed chair, *something*, amidst the flourishing wild garden, only finding the alpha's throne and nothing else.

"By the pool, maybe?"

"Sure."

We walked side-by-side after James briefly acknowledged Darius, the pair also shaking hands, though saying very little to one another. Settling at the edge of the clear blue water, I tugged off my shoes and dipped my feet in.

"No iron," James said offhandedly, and I nodded.

"I could tell." I dragged my legs through the cool water for a moment, then sighed, knowing it was best to just get right into this. "Can I ask—"

"I need to—" We both laughed, my cheeks flushing when we spoke over each other. With James a few feet to my left, Darius sat to my right, our bodies almost flush against one another. He set a hand on my lower back, studying the lily pads in silence. Clearly, he knew this was something I needed to do for myself, but I certainly couldn't have done it without him being there.

"I'll be glad to answer all of your questions," James told me, hands threaded together and resting on his lap. "But I need you to know something first."

I braced myself, but schooled my features as best I could. "Shoot."

"I didn't know your mother was pregnant when we parted ways," he insisted, and the pain of that knowledge read plainly across his darkening features. "I didn't know she had you. It wasn't until we met on the battlefield... I was flying over you, and I sensed that you were mine. I felt it in my heart, my soul, the same way I connected with my children on the days they were born." He chuckled softly, the darkness lifting as I grappled with the fact that he had other children—more half-siblings for me.

"It was like seeing the sunrise after an eternity of night. You took me right out of the battle."

"Sorry," I muttered, fighting back a smile. *I didn't know this man. Could I really take him at his word?*

"Don't be," James said, his emerald greens searching out mine. "It's one of the greatest feelings a shifter will ever experience, besides connecting with his mate. You gave me life out there, a piece of my heart I hadn't realized was missing. When I saw those vile creatures swarming in on you, I... I reacted. Whether you want a relationship with me or not, you're my blood, and I will defend you until my dying day."

And cue the waterworks again. I sniffed as subtly as I could, turning away to blink back the latest onslaught of tears. Physically, my body was still weak from the battle and recovering after the djinn attack. Emotionally, I was sure I'd crash hard when this conversation finished, no matter the outcome, and sleep well into tomorrow.

"And I'm not saying any of this because, I expect something from you," James told me. I exchanged a quick glance with Darius. His slight eyebrow twitch read as a *do we need to run for the hills?* kind of thing, to which I shook my head.

"I don't know what I'd have to give, even if you *did* expect something, honestly," I told my father, my wiggling toes, poking into the water's surface. "I'm a psychologist from New York City, when I'm not, you know, helping my half-brother lead a revolt against some genocidal fascist. I live in a one-bedroom apartment. I make a decent salary. I..." I looked to Darius. "I'm involved with a kind of super protective, shifter."

"*Very* protective," Darius murmured, taking my hand and grinning. Warmth trickled through me, and I was sure I positively glowed in the bastion of his support. I couldn't imagine an outsider looking at us and finding a chink in the armor for them to stab a knife through.

"I'll defend you and protect you because, you're my kin." James shifted on the spot, lips twitching into a gentle smile as he studied his clasped hands. "You're my blood. It's a shifter thing, to be so protective of our mates, our children, our family. It's instinct. We can't help it."

"I'm beginning to understand that," I admitted. Darius squeezed my hand gently a few seconds later, as if only then realizing that the comment was directed at him. Never in my life had I feared, adored, and fought so fiercely for one person before. The thought of harm coming to him in battle—it had driven me crazy. I had gone full on Mama Bear and Darius wasn't even *close* to being my cub. I couldn't imagine the bond between a shifter parent and child. If that innate pull was slowly taking hold of me as I embraced my other half, I couldn't imagine the powerful instinct to eviscerate anyone that threatened my lover or child. It must be overwhelming.

"I want you to know that I don't *want* anything from you," James told me. His expression shifted from soft to mildly panicked when my eyes widened, and he quickly backpedaled. "Not that I don't want a relationship, it's that I don't expect one right away, if you aren't willing to give it. I didn't come here anticipating you'd call me Dad and we'd have a beer together rehashing the good times. I..." He ran his fingers through his hair, clearly spiraling. "Don't feel pressured here. We can go at whatever pace you want... If you want a pace at all."

I bit my lip. I *did* want a relationship with him, but I needed all my concerns addressed first. None of my psychologist alarms were blaring so far, but I was a bit too jaded to simply usher him into my life. This would need work. It would take time.

"Did you love my mother?" My voice cracked. "She died giving birth to me."

Color flooded his cheeks, and he looked away, the bulge in his throat bobbing noticeably. *Did he know I'd been responsible for her death? Would he send me packing?*

"I loved your mother very much," he told me in a quiet, almost hoarse tone—like he was trying to keep it all together. "Our affair was brief and passionate. I didn't care that she was married… I thought she was my mate, the one I was destined for. My parents disapproved of my dating a supernatural being, and since I was preparing to step into the role of alpha, they forced me to choose between duty and love. In the end, I chose duty." James looked to me with shimmering eyes. "I've always regretted it, choosing as I did. I met my wife two years later. We wed. Had children. She died quite a few years ago. We never knew what happened…she was here one day, gone the next." His voice caught, and he cleared his throat. "I never forgot your mother."

Given the care he had put into the garden supposedly created by her, I could see that he kept her close. I reached back behind me and plucked a sprig of lavender, trailing the purple flowers at its head under my nose.

I'd always thought of lavender when I thought of my mother.

"Catelyn was an extraordinary person," James continued thoughtfully, and when I glanced up, he'd let a few tears fall and seemed to be in no hurry to wipe them away. "She was compassionate, witty, beautiful, intelligent… Which is very much my impression of you, Kaye."

I chuckled, though my throat felt tight, my chest too. On the verge of more tears—damn him. "That's very kind of you to say, but you don't know me at all."

"That's true, but everyone speaks so very highly of you." James nodded to Darius. "Particularly your man."

"He just knows better than to spill all my dirty secrets—"

"And I sincerely hope you don't blame yourself for what happened to your mother," James said quickly, his words stealing the breath right out of me. I stared down at the plucked lavender, my lower lip quivering. It stopped when he placed a hand on my shoulder, still keeping his distance as he whispered, "*I* certainly don't blame you. Anyone who does, is a fool, yourself included."

That earned a smile, and I hastily wiped my tears away. I then set my hand on top of his, finding it warm and worn, like a man who hadn't been afraid of manual labor over the years.

"Thank you," I murmured. He responded with a nod, eyes watery again.

"Of course."

We sat together in a contemplative silence for some time after, all three of us watching the waterfall roll down into the pool; a pool whose waters always remained relatively still—so as not to upset the lily pads. I would have thought my mind would be racing, flying through all the new information, processing it, compartmentalizing it in different corners of my brain for later. But there was nothing. The inside of my head was just... blank.

Happy. In some weird way, James had managed to put me at peace just by being honest and open. Neither my inner psychologist nor that prickly warning echo picked up on anything amiss with the man. While I still wasn't ready to call him Dad, I could accept that this was the start of something good.

"Can we come in yet? Have you guys had your moment?" A woman's voice broke our easy silence, and I turned back to find two faces peering at us from the doorway at the front of the hall.

"Leda," James chastised hastily, rising to his feet and walking toward her—before stopping and looking back at me. "I'm sorry. I told them you would need some time before meeting them, but they've been very impatient."

"Who?" Darius helped me up, my body ready for a nap anytime now, and I dried my calves and feet with a water wicking spell.

"My children. They've been very excited to meet you. I can send them away for—"

"No, no," I said as I smoothed my hands down my slouchy black shirt, its sleeves clipped up around my elbows. I looked like shit, still in the throes of healing, but if I could take the time to meet my father, I was certainly open to meeting my half-siblings. Particularly when they seemed so keen on meeting me.

James waved them in, and I remained next to Darius, watching as two grown dragon shifters hurried inside. The first was a woman—Leda, I assumed—and while she was taller than me, she had the same hippy figure that I did. She radiated strength and poise as she moved seamlessly through the garden, looking like she could feel equally at home on a football field *and* a ballet studio. Broad shoulders met a full figure, yet she barely made a sound with each passing step.

"I saw her fight in her dragon form," Darius murmured in my ear as she hurried closer. "She's fierce. A true alpha's daughter." He ran his hand up my back, resting it on my shoulder. "Like you."

Her hair was a few shades lighter than mine, and I noted a smattering of freckles across the middle of her face. The enormous smile she wore, bearing a set of perfectly white, straight teeth, was hard to miss, too.

"Kaye?" she asked, almost breathlessly. Behind, a lanky, though muscular man trailed after her—clearly the introvert to his sister's very palpable, extrovert, bearing the same freckled pattern over the bridge of his nose and our father's emerald green eyes. Hers were more hazel, though no less beautiful.

I hazarded a guess at her name, taking her hand when she offered it. "Leda?"

"Yeah, sorry." She laughed as we shook hands, a jolt of pleasant familiarity washing over me—like we had been waiting our whole lives to meet. "It's really nice to meet you. I hear you were a beast on the battlefield."

My cheeks warmed. I certainly hadn't *felt* like a beast out there. "Thank you. You know, Darius was just telling me the same about you."

"But *you* saved my best friend from gargoyles," Leda pressed, and I suddenly realized we were still holding hands. "Claire. She said you and your man here, saved her life. I'm in your debt."

"Hardly," Darius remarked. Slowly, Leda and I released each other's hands, though an invisible tether seemed to keep us connected. "There's no debt to be paid. Kaye and I just did what we were supposed to do... Defend our kind from a madman and his goons."

"Well, it isn't something I'll forget anytime soon," Leda told us, her smile wide and her eyes bright. "But, never mind that. I have a *sister*! I've always wanted one, but I just had a brother—"

"Hey," the man behind her piped up. "*Just* a brother?"

I caught James smiling to himself in the background, his arms crossed, and the warmth of his expression rubbed off on me. I grinned, unable to help myself.

"I'm Hudson," the man stated, stepping around his sister briefly to shake my hand. While I still felt that flutter of familiarity, it was stronger with Leda. Maybe I too had spent my whole life craving a sister, a *real* sister, but had to make do with a brother instead. Hudson had our father's build and kind eyes. His energy mellowed out Leda's somewhat, and I suspected under different circumstances, ones where I wasn't battling anxiety, my fears of meeting my family for the first time, and the remnants of djinn poison, we'd get along like two peas in a pod.

"I know you're only half dragon, but have you shifted yet?" Leda asked, positioning herself at the center of the conversation again. When my face fell slightly, she shook her head. "Oh, not that it's any of my business. It's just so strange meeting your kin in this form. We'd bond right away as dragons. It'd take some of the awkwardness out."

I stammered through a few incoherent words, then glanced back to Darius for help. From the look on his face, he was mildly unimpressed with Leda's sentiment, but I couldn't fault her. I could feel her enthusiasm for this, palpable and infectious; there was nothing wrong with wanting to speed up the process. *Only I couldn't shift. Or maybe I could. I just hadn't.* And somehow that made me feel less like James's daughter.

"We could go try it," Leda offered in the silence that followed, her eyes darting hastily between Darius and myself—as if realizing she'd fucked up. "It's a beautiful day for flying."

"I think Kaye could use some rest," James interjected while I fumbled for a response. The alpha strolled forward, then wrapped his arms around each of his children on either side of him. "She was poisoned by a freaking djinn. You don't shake that off in a few days. Perhaps, Darius, you might escort her somewhere quiet. I'll have something prepared for you, if you're hungry."

"That'd be nice," I managed, my voice quiet. "Thank you."

Darius took the hint and steered me out of the throne room. As amazing as it had been to meet my new family, it was starting to feel suffocating. There were still a lot of issues I had to confront about my heritage, and all the shifter politics, dynamics, and the whole shifting thing were just too much to stomach right now.

When we stepped outside, Cedric was waiting for us. Suddenly, I felt my knees give way, and I plummeted to the floor. Darius caught me before I made contact, and he scooped me into his arms, brushing off Cedric's offer of assistance with a look.

"You did really well in there," Darius told me as he cradled me in his arms and carried me away from the throne room, away from my newfound siblings and father, and toward what I could only hope was a place that would be calm and quiet. He kissed the tip of my nose when I forced a weak smile.

"Then why do I feel like I got hit by a bus?"

"Because you're a normal person with normal person emotions," he said, chuckling. "I'd be concerned if you were totally fine right now, to be honest."

He was right, of course. Everything I was experiencing—it was a natural, emotional response to what I'd gone through. Being a psychologist, you'd think I'd know that.

But like others in my profession, I always struggled to turn the microscope back on myself.

Luckily for me, I had my own personal sounding board, a shrink without the fees, right here. A shifter who adored me, but wouldn't hesitate to tell me the truth. Not anymore. I could read him too well.

And in the end, what else could a girl want?

"Do you think they have any chocolate around here?" I asked. "I could really go for a pound or two."

He laughed again and kissed me, this time capturing my lips in a slow, sensual kiss that I felt right down to my toes. A chill raced down my spine, banishing the unpleasant feelings away and welcoming in something better.

"I'll make it happen."

"Maybe some ice cream."

"Done."

"And some Chinese takeout..."

"Your wish is my command."

Our laughter echoed through the dark corridors—the sound was the best medicine in the world and lifted my very soul.

❧ 14 ❧

THREE DAYS LATER, my strength finally came back to me. The last of the djinn poison was out of my system, and I woke up feeling as though I could run a marathon without breaking a sweat.

I'd spent the last several days meeting with James, Leda, and Hudson separately, wanting to get to know them as individuals, rather than the familial clump the three represented in my mind. For the most part, it was just short conversations here and there, usually over a meal, or while I rested in my room, or back in the garden throne room designed by my mother. All three had kept to safe topics of conversation with me, though James had wanted to know the most about my life. Leda seemed happy to have a sister to chat with, while Hudson required a bit of work to pull conversation out of. In the end, I decided I liked them. This new little family suited me just fine, though I still wasn't ready to call James Dad yet, or see either of his children as my siblings.

But a blossoming friendship was there, and I expected it would develop further, the more time we spent together. Over breakfast that morning, Leda had suggested we go flying that afternoon with Darius and Quinn. I agreed to come just so I could watch dragons soar, a sight more beautiful than anything in the known universe, and dragged Catriona out too—though with Quinn there, she certainly didn't need much persuading. We all met at the rear castle gates at noon, then ventured out into the mountain range, questing ever higher along well-worn trails, headed for a peak.

"Alrighty," I said, grabbing Catriona by the elbow and falling back from the rest of the group. Both Darius and Quinn glanced back, noting our absence immediately, but after a pointed look from me, neither hung back to join us. I looked to Catriona and found her blushing, like she knew where the conversation was headed. "We need to talk."

"We've been talking all week," she said innocently, her gaze landing on a little gray bird that fluttered out of a stony crevice nearby. I scoffed.

"Not about what I *really* want to talk about." Darius had been my constant companion during my healing time, which I appreciated more than he would ever know, but his presence made it difficult to grill Catriona like I would have liked. "Out with it. *What* is happening with you and Quinn? Are you guys a thing?"

"Are we a *thing*?" Catriona giggled, the sound high and clear as a bell. "What is this, middle school?"

We linked arms, walking side-by-side at an even pace. "Don't try to change the subject."

She rolled her eyes, her blush darkening. "Kaye."

"Catriona." I tried to hide my grin, knowing I had her. Catriona had always been choosy with her heart. The thought that Quinn, of all people, might have captured it was a surprise.

"I just..." She shook her head as a smile bloomed across her face. "I just like him. He's... different. He's quiet but thoughtful, protective but not overbearing. I like embarrassing him, and I think he likes letting me. I don't know. I just like him."

"You said that," I noted. While I planned to tease her relentlessly, her reasons for crushing on Quinn made total sense to me. Catriona was sweet and bubbly, exuberant and kind. Quinn was a prickly, closed book, who probably needed someone exactly like my bestie to thrive. Someone who accepted him for exactly who he was—and *liked* him for who he was, prickliness and all.

"Oh, I don't know, Kaye." Her words flowed fast and true, as if spurred by excitement. "I've liked him from the moment I met him. Somehow, I just knew he was someone I ought to keep around. Someone I ought to invest my time in. I don't know *how* I knew. It was a gut instinct, I guess... a *feeling*."

My gaze darted to Darius's back. "I can understand that."

Slowly, anything about Darius that initially bothered me faded away. Suddenly he was a hot guy *and* a supportive shoulder to lean on. He made me laugh. He dried my tears. He made me feel strong and competent, even when I didn't think I had it in me. And when I thought back to when we first met, something had compelled me to let him in. Sure, I'd fought it, but when I considered the circumstances that thrust us together, it was all pretty absurd. I *could* have slammed the door in his face, honestly, whether he was the dark and handsome stranger I'd wanted to sleep with or not.

But *something* kept him in my life.

Like fate had nudged us together and we just... clicked. Despite the bickering, the fussing, and the headaches, I hadn't been apart from him for more than a day in months.

I glanced at my best friend. *Did she feel the same way about Quinn? Had fate played its hand again and brought two more souls together who needed each other?* As we walked alongside each other in a contemplative silence, I made a mental note to get to know Quinn better. If he did for Catriona what Darius did for me, then he too, was a worthy investment of my time.

Besides, I needed to give a best friend's blessing. While I had seen him fight Abramelin's minions and I had seen him fawn over Catriona, I needed just a *little* more before he earned my stamp of approval. I needed to know him, to understand him.

And, honestly, it was something I should have done already, he was Darius's brother. Hayden and I clicked right away, and while Hayden had flown home after the battle, with the other Sanctius dragons, he and I were on excellent terms.

Quinn? Well, it could be better.

It *would* be better. He was an important person in the lives of two of my favorite people, after all.

Catriona and I reached the mountaintop last. From our vantage point, we could see the entire range and everything around it. From the deep green forests on one side, to the glittering lake on the other, and well into the clear blue horizon in every direction. I unlinked my arm from Catriona's and cautiously stepped to the edge, filling my lungs with the crisp air the altitude offered. While the summer sun was as unrelenting as always, I was unusually comfortable in my skin.

The air crackled with excitement as the shifters discussed which routes to fly. Before any of the shifters could start stripping down to their underwear, heavy footsteps hurried up the path, gravel crackling underfoot.

"I apologize for the interruption, sir," Cedric announced as he appeared on the scene, nodding in deference to James, who gave the slightest nod in response. "But a messenger has arrived from the Sanctius clan. He requests a moment with Darius Thomas."

"Did he say anything that might suggest the kind of news he's carrying?" Darius asked as he strode toward Cedric. Quinn followed a few steps behind with a frown. The bald shifter shook his head, wearing the same distant, unreadable expression as he always did. I crossed my arms and hoped that it was just word from Hayden that he and the others had arrived safely.

"Right." Darius looked to his brother. "Stay. Have some fun. I'll be back shortly."

He turned away as Quinn started to protest, then shot me a quick glance before following Cedric back down the path. My gut told me to go with him, but my heart whispered to let him be. We might have been attached at the hip most of the time, but if it was private clan business he needed to hear, I didn't want to crowd him. So, I turned back to the group with a smile, hoping to distract Quinn from the steadily deepening frown dragging down his features.

"I'm sure it's nothing," I said. "Come on... Catriona and I came here to see some dragons!"

My best friend giggled, looping her arm around mine again, and just like that, the darkness eased out of Quinn's features.

"Maybe you'll join us sometime, Kaye," Leda insisted as she dragged her shirt over her head. "There's nothing like flying with your kin. It's the best high in the world."

"I can attest to that," Quinn added, wearing only a pair of boxer shorts. He neatly folded his clothes and placed them in a pile off to the side. I caught Catriona casting a shy glance over his body, which rippled with a subtle strength, tauter and leaner than Darius's muscular frame.

"Now, now," James sighed, then leaned over and pressed a chaste, barely there kiss to my cheek, "there's no pressure. If you are meant to shift, it'll happen when it happens."

I ran a hand through my loose hair, which caught in each gust of wind, making me wish I'd tied it back. "Thanks."

He shot me a wink as Leda pouted. Hudson rolled his eyes at his sister, then grinned when our gazes met. Clearly, he shared his father's patience. I didn't take Leda's enthusiasm for impatience, by any means. I took it for what it was: excitement. A willingness, a *desire*, to connect with me as shifters were meant to.

Once the four were stripped down to their underwear, with Catriona and I looking everywhere, but their semi-naked figures, they moved to the edge of our peaceful plateau—and jumped. My heart leaped up into my throat as I watched them fall, and Catriona gave a little frightened squeal and rushed to the edge, dragging me along with her. Seconds later, the rush of an enormous white dragon raced by, shooting up into the air, sending us tumbling onto our backsides. Three more figures followed, trailing after the much larger leader of the group, their cries a symphony that made my heart sing.

I assumed the largest was James. He was pure white with silver tipped wings, a gloriously beautiful dragon. Catriona and I briefly lost sight of him when he passed through the snowy clouds that dotted the otherwise clear sky. Next in line was a dragon only a bit smaller than Darius, one I knew intrinsically to be Leda. She was bright red, like the stripe of a candy cane, with white marks across her four massive feet, all of which were tipped with sharp, black talons.

Bringing up the rear was Quinn's navy blue dragon, the various other hidden colors of his scales glittering in the sunlight. Catriona couldn't take her eyes off him—not that I could blame her. He flew next to the smallest dragon of the bunch: Hudson. As the youngest, I assumed he would also be the smallest: a little olive green dragon, one distinct color from top to bottom, with only a few spikes along his back. Those teeth though... When he roared, I noted that his dragon body still needed to grow into his razor-sharp set of teeth.

"They're so..." Catriona opened and closed her mouth, as though struggling for words as we watched them soar. I nodded, unable to wipe the smile from my face.

"Beautiful?"

"Exquisite."

"Agreed."

We perched at the edge of the plateau, legs dangling over the brink of a rocky abyss—a good hundred-foot drop, if we slipped. The usual fear of hanging over a great distance wasn't there, mostly because I couldn't tear my gaze away from the dragons above. I closed my eyes for a moment, letting their song fill my soul, breathe life into my marrow, before staring up dreamily.

My inner voice had been lulled into silence too, though I felt this *pull*, this undeniable need to be with them. I yearned to jump, to soar, to race alongside my father, my newfound siblings. I longed to be included, to be welcomed into the fold as one of them. Heart hammering inside my chest, I lifted a hand, tracing James's flight with my finger—then stared, wide-eyed, at my arm when something rippled beneath my skin. Swallowing hard, I brought my hand back to me, and swore something skittered along beneath my skin again. Adrenaline pounded through me, illuminating every limb, every fiber. A wave of nausea followed, yet I'd never felt more alive. My senses heightened without me calling upon them.

Was this...?

Was Leda right? Being in the presence of my kin... Perhaps it was drawing something out of me, something long dormant, something that yearned to join the chorus of cries thundering across the sky.

Could I possibly be on the verge of—

"Oh, Darius is back."

I turned away at Catriona's words, and the feeling rapidly subsided. Blinking hard, I pushed up to my feet, ready to hold Darius's clothes for him—I could only imagine he longed to join the other dragons soaring overhead. However, my smile faded when I caught the look on his face. He lifted hollow, distant eyes to mine, then slowly turned and made his way back down the path. Biting my lower lip, I hurried off after him, catching up a few moments later.

"Darius?" I caught his arm, stopping him, and slowly waited for him to face me. The whites of his eyes had turned faintly red, and he felt stiff within my grasp. My heart dropped.

"Word from home," he said thickly. "My father is dead."

I said nothing—because what could I possibly say? I'm sorry? No one wanted to hear that when someone had passed on. *I'm sorry* never fixed anything. It didn't alleviate the guilt, the pain, the agony of loss. So, instead, I stood up on the tips of my toes and hugged him, as hard as I could, until finally his body lost its stiffness and collapsed against me. He trembled as I stroked his hair, but as far as I could tell, no tears fell.

Typical Darius. I knew he would grieve in whatever way seemed right on his own time, whether I saw it or not.

"I must go home," he told me, his voice hoarse when we broke apart. He raked his fingers through his hair and shifted his gaze elsewhere, everywhere but to me. "You should stay. Be with your family."

I shook my head. "Not on your life."

"Kaye. Stay with your—"

"*You* are my family," I snapped, poking him hard in the chest until he looked at me. "Don't you dare think about leaving me here. I'll come after you. You know I'm just as stubborn as you are."

He gave a weak chuckle in response. "I suppose that's true. But you've only just connected with them. Don't you—"

"We have all the time in the world to get to know each other," I argued, pushing all thoughts of the ramifications of Khalon Thomas's death to the back of my mind. Surely, Darius had a thousand thoughts racing through his head, too. For now, all that mattered was that my dragon survived this—and I would be right by his side to see him through it. "Seriously. I'm coming with you."

"But—"

"We do this *together*," I said forcefully, taking his hand in both of mine and squeezing, "or not at all."

Using his own words against him—I just couldn't help myself. Darius lifted his gaze to the horizon, jaw clenching for a moment. I could see it all, the weight of this news. It would drown him, if he let it. Thankfully, my generous hips made me *very* buoyant. I wouldn't let him splash around for long.

"Together it is then," he said, exhaling deeply. His fingers laced around mine. In the distance, the bellowing of four great dragons filled the air. Darius slowly sank to the ground, his head in his hands, and I followed, holding him to me in the shade of the mountainside.

"Together," I whispered.

For whatever the future held, darkness or light, I couldn't imagine it without my dragon. Because I loved him. I'd stand by him. Always.

~

158

THANK YOU FOR READING **MAGIC BURN!**
Read book 3...MAGIC BLAZE!

GET A FREE SEDONA VENEZ BOOK!

https://sedonavenez.com/free-book

WANT FREE SEDONA VENEZ BOOKS?

Sign up for Sedona Venez's Newsletter and receive FREE BOOKS. In addition to the free stories, you will also get special pricing, exclusive previews and news of new releases.

GET A FREE SEDONA VENEZ BOOK!

Join Sedona's mailing list to be the first to know of new releases, free books, special prices and other author giveaways.

https://sedonavenez.com/free-book

ABOUT THE AUTHOR

USA TODAY BESTSELLING AUTHOR SEDONA VENEZ lives in New York City with her hot ex-military hubby—hooah—and their fur babies. She loves writing sizzling, sexy intricate stories about strong but broken characters who push limits, overcome their fears and risk it all for love.

Sedona loves to connect with readers!
www.sedonavenez.com